BACH
AND THE HEAVENLY CHOIR

JOHANNES RÜBER

BACH

AND THE HEAVENLY CHOIR

TRANSLATED FROM THE GERMAN BY
MAURICE MICHAEL

THE WORLD PUBLISHING COMPANY

CLEVELAND AND NEW YORK

Library of Congress Catalog Card Number: 57-5888

FIRST EDITION

FIRST PUBLISHED IN MUNICH BY
ALBERT LANGEN-GEORG MÜLLER
UNDER THE TITLE
DIE HEILIGSPRECHUNG DES JOHANN SEBASTIAN BACH

HC157

BACH
AND THE HEAVENLY CHOIR

THE BACKS OF HIS HANDS had the pigmentation of the Mediterranean peoples, yet he came from elsewhere, the first Pope for a long time not to be an Italian. He who for the last seven years had occupied the papal throne was a man of the Basques, the people who inhabit the Atlantic coast on either side of the Pyrenees; his mother tongue was French.

Pope Gregory laid his violin aside. His hands slid down, rather limp and tired from the intensive playing to which he had devoted one hour of the afternoon. The last notes died away. His playing was artistically perfect: he had been trained by Spanish and French teachers, and his original intention had been to take up music.

Sisters Clara and Raphaela started slightly; an expectant expression appeared on their faces, pointed and still youthful looking beneath their caps. Attuned to the Holy Father's every movement, the question "What will he do now?" again trembled on their lips.

After meals and after playing—he never let a day pass without practicing—the Pope liked complete relaxation. There was no reading nor praying then; his object was utter rest for his body. This was slender and of medium stature, and he made a fine figure with his gray head the color of melting snow. At these times he walked in the gardens or went for a drive through the streets of the Eternal City, along the Via Appia or round the city by the side roads. Somewhere he would stop the car and gaze out through the window, his slightly hooked nose pressed against the glass.

Ernest, the chauffeur, saw a side of the Pope which others never saw, not even his Secretary of State, young Cardinal Hopkins. The Pope loved driving, whether slowly or fast. Behind Ernest's round back he felt perfectly safe. Nobody else gave him such a feeling of security. Ernest had been the driver of the bus that plied between the market town and the Benedictine monastery in Haute Bourgogne where Gregory had lived as a monk until his election. He, for whom a cell had then been room enough, must have found the Vatican cramping at the beginning, for he soon began to make these secret escapes, either in the afternoon or in the evening when the sun was going down behind Ostia and there was much red in the sky above the City of the Seven Hills. Requiring a safe driver for his car, he had sent for Ernest, who drove for the *Société des Cars et Autobus* of Bourg and Besançon.

They were an obsession, these drives outside the city, along the smooth roads where the wind came warm off the sea or blew down fresh from the hills, with the windows of the car open, and Ernest the only witness of those remarkable sayings to which he learned to pay heed, as did the black-and-white-clad nuns in the Vatican: "It gives Us resolution," the Pope cried, "like soldiers when they march against the enemy . . . This wind! It blows all business from your head!"

But he had never flown. He deplored the fact to the young

Cardinals when they came to Rome by air. When Cardinal Hopkins returned from America, where he had had to intervene in a dispute between the Confessions, the first thing about which Gregory had inquired was not the result of the negotiations, but what the flight had been like, how the thunderclouds had looked, how everything had looked, the clouds from above, the earth from above, and, since Hopkins had flown part of the way by night, whether the world of the stars had looked different up there than it did from down below.

Outside the city were great tenements, giant honeycombs which stood dazzlingly white on the Campagna when the sun shone, and down which the water streamed in loathsome long streaks when it rained. The Pope's way took him past these buildings, and they made him shake his head. It was a grief to him that he had only the one life, that he could not intervene, was not able to relieve distress, had not the means to reprimand governments when they did not discharge their duties to the full. It was a thing anyone would have wanted; and there were grounds for accusing the Pope of inactivity. He was, indeed, a strange man: so far he had propounded no dogma and undertaken no canonization; he had produced no social epistle, no fulmination against the tyrants of whom there were still plenty ruling a variety of countries up and down the world; and doubt of his diplomatic abilities had long been openly voiced.

He himself suffered most from the fact that he had only the one talent, for by nature he was an artist. He readily realized his deficiencies and was continually trying to make them good, but he had not yet brought himself to undertake any major action to which all his theologians would have given their united assent. He still had a number of remarkable ideas, expressive of pious eagerness to serve his God, and these he pondered day after day as he used to do in the Benedictine monastery. But none demanded to be put into effect; and so no one knew of them.

He was enlarging upon one of these favorite ideas that afternoon as, his violin laid aside, he stood looking thoughtfully through the tall window at the roofs of Trastevere which were autumnally beflagged with thin pennants of smoke. The white columns rose up steeply into the blue heavens, slightly interweaving with each other, just as a short while before the partita of Johann Sebastian Bach had slipped through the pompous old Vatican room that was the Pope's music room—had soared, its notes also interweaving, dancing, and tripping, with movement and festive graces.

Pope Gregory thought in French. "Jean-Sébastien," he thought.

"Saint Jean-Sébastien," he added.

It was like the daring thought of a boy dreaming dreams and it made him smile. It was one of those thoughts of his which, if he ever spoke them aloud, made most of his theologians shake their heads and in one or two aroused real concern.

"What would Hopkins think of that, I wonder?" thought Gregory.

He stood there by the window, folded his arms, and looked down at the roofs of Rome; his eyes blinked behind the thick lenses of his glasses, which gave his face an expression of helplessness.

"Hard to say. Perhaps he would agree. Because it was me. Perhaps. But strict Monsignore Mancini—or Cardinal Platoni —or even the two nuns at my door . . ."

He did not speak his thought aloud but hugged it to himself. He put the violin in its case; the black velvet felt as soft as the fur of a cat, yet he pulled his hand away as though it had

received an electric shock and held it up, index finger admonish-
ingly raised, and an amused yet also startled smile on his lips.
Then he closed the lid and, stepping lightly, left the room.
Past the waiting Sisters, and down the steps, he made his way
to the garden, where his figure disappeared among the harsh
greens of the oaks and cypresses, breaking the threads of gossamer that still remained from summer as he went.

CHAPTER 2

H IS CALL to the papal chair was like a fairy tale. He had never been a secular priest. Until his election he had lived in complete seclusion in a French Benedictine monastery, where for many years he had been the organist and latterly its abbot.

Then the previous Pope had died. The world knew that there was only one fit successor, one on whom the Cardinals could rely, who was strong enough to hold the helm of the Church. The Cardinals seemed agreed on the importance of the key position occupied by the American Cardinal in the politics of the Church and of the world. Also, no secret was made of their assumption that the American Catholics, for whom no other candidate but their Cardinal existed, would gain in numbers and power the day their Cardinal was elected. They could anticipate an incalculable sequence of conversions among American Protestants, many of them people in the most influential spheres. And yet the Cardinals suddenly let this unique chance go. No one rightly knew why. It was said, though, that shortly before his death the late Pope had made certain suggestions and given advice which made it appear that the election of the American would be dangerous and undesirable. Support grew quickly for this view, which was held most strongly by certain of the Vatican theologians, in particular by Cardinal Platoni, one of the closest associates of the late Pope. New names were soon being mentioned, among them Platoni's; also a Chinese Cardinal and an Indian. There was mockery and ridicule, and discord threatened. Politicians, European and American, Western and Oriental, began to take a hand. With the previous Pope dead and the Cardinals assembled in Rome to elect a new one, the situation, though garbed in the democratic mufti of our age, became medieval; it might almost have been set in the Renaissance, and to all who took part, and to those who didn't, it was a grotesque pantomime.

Balloting went on for a long time. The chimney smoked blackly.

Most of the votes cast were blank. No agreement was reached until in the end the calmer members of the consistory suggested a solution which, in its effect, was as medieval and Renaissance-like as the cause of the whole dispute. This step that the Church finally felt itself compelled to take was nothing but a flight from reality. The Cardinals agreed on the strange idea of not having a diplomat. They were not going to elect a Peter, but a contemplative Matthew. And so after weeks of painful consideration and of voting without reaching a decision, the men of the consistory finally agreed for the first time since anyone could remember to elect not a Cardinal, but some other important churchman. Names were put forward, those of bishops, scholars, monks, among them that of a French abbot, no longer young, but strong enough to hold the office for a year or two.

Father Severin had attracted attention with a number of papers. They were pure theory, neither polemical nor apologetic, in the direct line of the medieval writings of men like St. Thomas. Mostly, however, Severin had been occupied with art.

Before his election as abbot he had been organist of his monastery. The monks had made him their abbot because of his appearance, his pious simplicity, and his learning; the real qualities of leadership were not in him, though he possessed great latent powers of spiritual healing. This man the Cardinals unanimously elected Pope. A delegation went to fetch him from his monastery. The Cardinals drove up the winding road of the monastery valley in fast, silent, shiny limousines bearing the plates of many countries. They alighted in their resplendent crimson.

The abbot did not let himself be intimidated by the crimson-clad guests come to his monastery to take him back to Rome in triumphal procession more legendary than any since the great age of Christian architecture—a mighty testimony to which was Severin's own Burgundian monastery. He listened sympathetically to what the Cardinals had to say, nodding his assent. What the Cardinals had feared never happened: the abbot gave his consent unhesitatingly. It did not occur to him that he might refuse. . . .

He had two lauds sung, two primes—for the delegation had arrived at the hour of the tierce—three sexts, and three vespers, and so one morning between the third matin and third laud he left his monastery and drove away to Rome in a magnificent limousine that meanwhile had been cleansed of the dust of the Burgundian highways.

They had elected him unanimously, been enthusiastic about their choice which soon found popular favor. How was it that later they came to regret it? It was no senile old man they had elected. Neither limousine nor purple impressed him, any more than did the experience of the aged Cardinals who proffered their friendship. He preferred to make a couple of trustworthy friends among the younger ones.

One of these was an Englishman, Cardinal Hopkins. He was a tall, thin man with bright eyes and fair hair. His profile was the firmest that had been encountered in the Vatican for a decade; yet, in his face there was an element of perpetual unrest, playing mostly in the inner corner of the eyes, at the side of the bridge of the nose, and round the mouth above the chin. His appointment had not been on Gregory's initiative; Hopkins' name had been one of those put forward the first time candidates were suggested for receiving the cardinal's hat. Those whom Gregory had to appoint were baked of his predecessor's dough, as the popular saying went, and Gregory knew nothing of any of them. Even Hopkins, who had previously been a Vatican prelate, he had scarcely even seen during the short time he had been there. He noticed him when he gave him the crimson. They had a talk together, and Gregory appointed him Cardinal Secretary of State, instead of Cardinal Platoni as had originally been intended. At the same time he nominated him the new titular bishop of the Church of the Holy Cross of Jerusalem, in the neighborhood of St. John Lateran, the Pope's church.

This action was the first to arouse the indignation of some of the older Cardinals.

"What attracts Your Holiness about this Englishman?" asked Cardinal Platoni, the man with the longest Vatican experience, and latterly in the inner conclave. He was, as he was called, the father of the Mediterranean, *il padre del Mediterraneo*, the person in the Vatican who dealt with the petitions of the Romanic peoples.

"At least," said Gregory in reply to Platoni's almost malicious question, "he is not an American."

"That would have been better," Platoni replied.

"We rather like the English," said the Pope, looking almost gaily at the Cardinal through his strong glasses.

"In general?" asked Platoni.

"At least in particular," said the Pope. "They have character."
And then with a smile he corrected himself, to get in ahead of
Platoni. "At any rate their faces have."

And half jokingly, half in earnest, he gestured across the roofs
of Rome to where, in the distance, screened by huge nodding
pine trees, ran a piece of ancient battlemented wall, where the
pyramid of Cestius stood in blue marble in front of the brown
arched gateway through which the Apostle Paul went to Ostia
when he took ship for Spain, and again later when he was taken
to the place of his execution.

"And often they have justified the name they bear, those
Anglo-Saxons, or so it seems to us," said Gregory. "There have
often been faces of angels among them. Shelly, Keats . . ."

"Oh," said the Cardinal, startled, and his raised hand gave a
slight jerk, "faces which in the end vice has ravaged." And as he
said this he thought almost disgustedly: "So the Holy Father
points in the direction of the Protestant cemetery."

Cardinal Platoni, a man with a strong hand that was more
often blessed than blessing, and who held admirably strong
views, was known far and wide as an opponent, especially in the
Romanic lands entrusted to his care, of the Protestant error that
claimed for itself the right of truth as much as did Rome.
Gregory's predecessor had repeatedly had to reprimand him and
to mitigate his zeal, which at times was so great as to harm the
authority of the Church.

"Now, Platoni," said the Pope, smiling, "don't you like the
poets either?"

"Dante," said the Cardinal.

"We can tell you in friendly confidence," Gregory said, "that
We imagine God as being only just a little more understanding
and benevolent than are the poets, who of all mortals have the

greatest and wisest understanding and forgiveness for us, or at least who ought to have . . ."

Cardinal Platoni smiled. He forced himself to. Then he bowed slightly and withdrew, and as he went, in a gesture of despondency, he exhaled through clenched teeth the breath he had been holding while the Holy Father spoke. Not till the great door closed behind him did he open his eyes, which at the end he had blindly closed.

Eventually most of Gregory's theologians were wagging their heads over all his pronouncements and decisions, and only a few, whose favor he had unwittingly won, were in agreement with him. These, headed by Cardinal Hopkins, were nonetheless in the minority. The populace, taking its cue from Ernest, the chauffeur, and the two nuns, Clara and Raphaela, gave the Pope the veneration which it has for all Popes.

Gregory's was an unsophisticated mind. If he ever ventured into the world of politics, it was with the most anxious diffidence. He made no secret of his ignorance of matters of contemporary history, and he had not the least intention of posing as the great man capable of dealing with dangerous situations. Yet whatever he did was done with warmth, and to everyone's surprise always proved successful. This was because he never undertook too much. He disregarded the warnings of his admirers and put himself in touch directly with the camp of the enemy; yet he did so in such a delicate way that they could not repulse him. He even talked with the leaders of the apparently most unyielding, left-orientated parties and found a ready hearing. All his arrangements were verbal ones. He wanted no epistles, scarcely made a covenant, and although he was not able to prevent the historical misfortunes which occurred after his time, he at least helped to postpone them. During his reign no world-shaking disaster occurred.

All the same there was justification for those who expected clear decisions from a Pope, and who demanded that he should set up landmarks in the history of the Church to help fortify the belief of mankind. They wanted tonics of dogma, expressions of opinion, canonizations. In short, they longed for the fireworks which this pious, introspective, and yet unfailingly candid man so stubbornly and apparently remissly failed to provide.

CHAPTER 3

SUCH IS THIS AGE that, when one of the most important men of the Lutheran Church, Hammerschmied, Bishop of Hamburg, received a letter in the handwriting of the Pope, it was a thing to marvel at. How had this man come to be singled out? The Bishop was reputedly level-headed: he had been born in the Harz Mountains, though for several decades now he had lived in north Germany, and thus he embodied both the German characters—the introspective, contented nature of the inhabitant of hilly or mountainous country, and the farseeing, ponderous disposition of those who had to face the harsher aspects of life in the plain, and whose bishop he was. Add to that the salt of the sea. He lived in the neighborhood of the coast, near ebb and flood, at the point where the broad Elbe, that relative of the sea, had just freed itself from the trough of the river bed.

The Pope's letter came as a Christmas greeting, a short time before our story begins, and it greatly astonished the Bishop. Yet, however much he turned it over and over in his hands, no doubt was possible: the seal was genuine. Then it seemed to him that the thing to do would be hastily to summon a church

synod and to lay the letter before it. What was one to expect of
Gregory the Remarkable, from whom no one any longer looked
for anything? An attack against Lutherans? His almost open
antagonism to Cardinal Platoni made that seem unlikely. Or—
Hammerschmied wondered—was the Pope entertaining plans
for a reunion? In either event the letter did not concern just
the Bishop alone.

Nevertheless, what Bishop Hammerschmied finally did was
as prosaic as the manner of the letter's arrival: he opened it. As
befitted the democratic lack of scarlet of our age, the letter had
come by ordinary post; although still smelling of oranges and
lemons it had not been brought by a courier from the Vatican,
but by the local postman. The Bishop opened it.

He read it hastily, running an eye over it, and was at once
moved by its purport though without fully comprehending it.
What a delightful surprise! In his hand he held a little work of
art. He read it twice, thrice, turned it upside down to relish the
small and lovely script without its meaning. He read it again.
And then, as should be the case with a delicate little work of art,
tears came into his eyes, from which all perplexity had slowly
faded.

No one was told anything of the contents of the letter. It was
known that the Pope had written to the Bishop, for the Vatican
announced briefly and concisely in its wireless bulletin, doing
so in the same terms as it announces the reception in audience of
a second-class statesman, a poet, or an artist: "Pope Gregory XIX
received the poet N. N. in audience lasting a quarter of an
hour." Then people wonder: "What can the two have said to
each other? N. N. is anything but a Catholic."

This, then, was the announcement: "The Pope has sent a
Christmas greeting to the evangelical Bishop of Hamburg."

That started the speculation. People jumped to the conclu-

sion: of course Gregory, for whose contribution to Church
history people had waited so long, and who had been made far
too much of a legendary figure after his compromise election,
was just the man to conceive the idea of reuniting the Church
which had been divided for more than five hundred years.

No one dared to predict how he intended to put this into
practice. There was no evidence of his possessing the energy.
No, it was scarcely likely that anything would come of such a
dream. And then, after all, Gregory was an artist. Of course, he
was the Holy Father, but scarcely a Peter in charge of the keys.
You could not expect anything that would go down to history
from a man of his diplomatic stature. The Church had no great
enemy at the time, it was true, but if it had had he would have
found no very powerful opponent in Gregory.

"The Church sleeps very softly beneath his hand," one or two
Vatican officials, who were inclined to scoff, confided to visitors.

"Even when he plays the violin?" they were asked.

"His personal Sisters, Clara and Raphaela, enjoy a nap every
afternoon outside the Pope's music room. When he stops playing, they wake with a start."

Cardinal Platoni, however, said: "A lovable, a wonderful man,
the Holy Father. I imagine the most important figure in the
Vatican for centuries. But he's certainly not thinking of a union
of the Confessions, of which one is the true Church. . . . The
Protestants have no head who could be a partner to the Holy
Father. That is why we regard the Holy Father's Christmas
letter to the Lutheran Bishop as a private matter."

"But what might it really signify?"

"A whim?" suggested Platoni interrogatively.

"Or did the Lutheran write first?"

"I have no information about that," said Platoni, raising his
hand briskly. "It would be perfectly possible. Perhaps the Bishop

was complaining about us, and the Pope was smoothing things out. A few well-intentioned words. A sort of diplomatic ruse to get around the situation . . ."

The Bishop of Hamburg kept the contents of the letter to himself. Only one or two intelligent guesses came near the truth which, as always, was perfectly simple and straightforward. The Bishop of Hamburg was considered a musical scholar of note; he was well known as an expert on the works of Johann Sebastian Bach. It was on his initiative that during the last few decades those great cycles of cantatas had been held which had caused the Lutheran liturgy to experience a renaissance.

The Bishop maintained silence as far as the public was concerned. But he replied to the Pope at once, which was proof that the correspondence was not to be taken too gravely; for otherwise the conscientious man would have been forced to give lengthy consideration to his reply. The Pope received his reply during the Christmas festival.

The composition of the reply showed how conscientious a man the Bishop of Hamburg was. He sat up all one night with his daughter, a strange being with long coppery-brown hair and large, ardent brown, almost southern eyes, whom people would see running through the foggy or sunny streets of Hamburg, where the wind blows in from the sea, on her way to sing in the cantata choir or to her piano lessons—and always with a piece of music, usually of Johann Sebastian Bach, tucked under her arm. The Bishop's house was one of the few in that busy city where they played the harpsichord. Luise Hammerschmied always played that instrument for the famous performances of the cantatas. There was a special reason why the Bishop of Hamburg now felt compelled to this act of conscientiousness: in that night of vigil before he wrote his reply, which he did the following morning, he and his daughter together went through the Fifth Brandenburg Concerto. Their faces shone, the world forgotten. At intervals, while Luise earnestly practiced the cadenza of the first movement where the orchestra leaves the delicate harpsichord in the lurch, till the playing of her remarkably flexible hands was near perfection, the Bishop would run to the window, pull back the curtains and stare out into the clear winter's night. Bare tree trunks and the conifers in the garden shut the house off from the distant lights of the city. The stars were exceedingly bright that night and seemed to have moved close up to the glass. Cold weather had started just before Christmas with a northeaster, the most bitter of all winter winds. There was a sharp edge to the wind this evening, something fierce and hostile about it which ripped the mind open as it pressed crackling against the glass. By day, however, the sky was as blue as in the south; the sun shone between the houses and shot its slender shafts over an almost summer-dusty countryside, on which no snow had fallen. All water was frozen over, the Elbe, the Alster, the coastal waters, the shallows; the offshore islands were all cut off. Sun and moon both ruled, it is true, but the moon was one phase the stronger. Those were beautiful nights, yet theirs was a cruel beauty; for when the wintry earth did not have the protective cover of the clouds, the cold stars were to be feared more than the waves of the sea, more than the sand of the desert.

"There," suddenly said Luise, the air filled with her firm and delicate playing, "that must be right."

And she played on beyond the clear boundary of the cadenza, to where all at once the orchestra is there again and both join forces to conclude the exultation in major key.

Then the Bishop walked across to his daughter and as she drew a deep breath and straightened up from the slender keys of the harpsichord, he showed her the letter. He did so even at the risk, which suddenly occurred to him, of its leading his strangely overstrung but by no means pious daughter toward the Church of Rome; the thing was lovable and human enough for that.

Luise promised secrecy and read the letter, looking at it from the side, for she dared not take it from her father. She too was at once fired with enthusiasm for the poetry of it, uttered little sounds of delight, made as if to take the letter, but drew back; and as her father, highly pleased, laid it in the palm of her hand she said: "And that sentence at the end: 'And, also, We are not quite sure how the harpsichord should play the cadenza in the Fifth Brandenburg Concerto, and a little illustration would . . .' Isn't he sweet?"

CHAPTER 4

IN THE SPRING the Hamburg Cantata Society went on tour.
For the first time, it was to give concerts in the countries of
southern and western Europe. The tour had long been planned.
Performances of baroque works in Holland, Belgium, France,
and Spain had been announced; yet, suddenly, on instructions
from the Bishop of Hamburg, the itinerary was changed and
bags and instrument cases, Bach trumpets, cellos, and double
basses, instead of being taken to the Ostend train were put
aboard the Syracuse express. They were going to Italy, and the
Bishop was going with them.

The Cantata Society headed south. Leaving the narrow confines of the north it passed through the territories of Germany;
past the Harz Mountains, crossing Protestant country where
churches with colorless windows stand beneath mighty lime
trees and oaks, where once the cantors worked; up the River
Main they went and into Catholic country, where crosses and
madonnas stand by the roadside, where churches have colorful
windows and deep rich pictures. To Munich. Through Alpine
valleys, and across the Brenner. Down the Adige from the
region of snows into the now only lightly snow-covered valleys

of the Tridentine Alps with their bold cypresses beneath brown cliffs on which lay a glow of morning sunlight. Past the gray, mortared stones of the city of Trent, where once the Catholic opponents of the Reformation met together to draw up the new order of hard and strict resolve, that in the end was to complete the divorce between the piety that was realistic, holy, and temperate, and that which was salutary and imaginative, between Christian freedom and Christian organization. On through the narrow breach of the Adige and out into the plain of Lombardy, still wintry and bare and strewn with lime. In the tracks of kings wanting the imperial crown of the Holy Roman Empire, in the tracks of poets wishing to see real laurels, in the tracks of Johann Sebastian Bach, who, though in the flesh he never left his North, yet in spirit had been to fetch the ripe fruits of the South, before he built the mountain of his cantatas and fugues in the lowlands of north Germany and above the hills between the Werra and the Oder. In the tracks of Heinrich Schütz, of Mozart and Gluck. Past Venice and on to Florence. In Tuscany, the last of the tunnels behind them, they found a mild blue sky. Into the home of physically pure, baroque music; to the abodes of Gregory the Great, Palestrina, Frescobaldi, Monteverdi, and Antonio Vivaldi. And to the altar of St. Peter's, from which Johann Sebastian obtained his most beautiful, his greatest strains and themes without ever having been there.

Thus they reached Rome, where they were to start their series of concerts. The Pope had invited them and Bishop Hammer-schmied had accepted. The first performance was to be in the Sistine Chapel. Artists had played before Popes often enough, great ones, minor ones, composers, virtuosi. There was no special significance about the Pope wishing to hear the cantata singers. Afterward there was to be another performance in the

concert hall for the public of Rome. Tickets for the two evenings had long been sold out. The Germans found posters on
the house walls of Rome announcing their program in large
Gothic letters. It was printed large on kiosks, pillars, gateways,
and walls: "Vocal and Instrumental Concert of Works by
Johann Sebastian Bach." The singers clustered in front of these
posters enjoying their young fame.

In Rome Bishop Hammerschmied behaved as a person of no
importance. That was what he wished. He had accompanied his
choir and musicians as far as Rome, and he was himself going
to sing in the concert in the Vatican. He wanted to see the
Pope, to see how he received his present. After that he would
go back home.

He was wearing a gray raincoat. With his daughter at his
side, her brown hair enveloped in a gay scarf, he walked through
midday Rome. From the bridge of Fabricius to the Tiber island
they had the dome of St. Peter's straight in front of them. Now
and again one of them would pass some remark. Slowly they
lost that silent surrender to unfamiliar objects. Their first few
impressions of that open city had been that it was uncommunicative, almost hostile; then a couple of moving encounters
had put them in conciliatory mood. Alongside the Tiber, opposite two heathen temples once dedicated to Vesta and Fortuna,
they had found the little church of Maria in Cosmedin and had
gone in. Quiet encompassed them, twilight and the slight
breathing of the God who let Himself be addressed there. Slowly they walked past the golden lateral niches, with which later
ages had made the little church also a place of gold and splendor. There, beneath the flat ceiling of the basilica, between the
black pillars of long-past ages, among the shadowy frescoes,
they felt challenged to pray. The Bishop did not resist. He
thanked God for being so uncomplicated, so easy to apprehend.

How good it was to be able to visit Him in that place, so small inside, away from the traffic of the streets, behind white ruined temples of the gods of antiquity.

They stayed for half an hour. Then the bells of the campanile drove them out. It was twelve o'clock and the hour when the custodian closed the church. The Lord was allowed a midday break.

Luise said: "Pan's hour."

Still caught up in the church's atmosphere, the Bishop replied: "The simple makes you devout. How perplexed those who built that little church would be in the cathedral of St. Peter's, beneath that boundless vault and among all that cold marble and lavish gold."

And as they walked past the sentries standing at the Vatican gate in antiquated uniform, with rifles and fixed bayonets, Hammerschmied said: "And Christ would say to these sentries: 'Put up again thy sword.'"

"What things you think of!" Luise cried out at that, almost reproachfully. "I'm not thinking any more now. I am just seeing everything, and my mind is storing the things my eyes have seen: bambinos, girls, lemons, the evergreen of the cypresses. Oh, Father, I don't think I shall be finished with this city for a long time. . . ."

They took a bus to the Gate of St. Paul, where they wanted to visit the Protestant cemetery. Again it was quiet. The gate was as high as the wall which surrounded that secluded spot. Mighty pine trees towered above the wall, screening it and its battlements. The graves lay at the foot of the old city walls; on some of the stones lay the shadow of cypress boughs, others had mimosa flowering over them. In those old days when the citizens of Rome stopped foreign Protestants from burying their dead within the city, this place still lay outside the walls. Now the ancient wall had lost its significance, had long since been outflanked by the houses of the modern city.

The Bishop pointed to a water conduit splashing out from the wall near the gate. A young crow had perched on the rim of the basin, and its yellow beak was pecking at the many falling drops, so that they splashed and sparkled round the bird's plumage. The noise of traffic, of which there was a junction outside the San Paulo Gate, was almost entirely banished from that peaceful place.

They found Keats's grave.

"Water again," said the Bishop. "Here lies one whose name is writ in water. . . ."

"Here," said Luise, "lie Goethe's son, Shelly, and Keats . . . You know, Father, I can't find a lot to like about the Roman Church. People can feel at home in any wayside chapel. That keeps my eyes busy like the flame of a candle at which you can look for hours and dream. And yet for me the ear is the thing, and the murmur of the sea is more powerfully familiar. Bach's name too is a symbol for water."

The Cantata Society was a little closed community, almost a family; several of its members were married to each other, and in the orchestra father played beside son, brother by sister, and betrothed by betrothed. And as they filed into the Sistine Chapel they all reacted in the same way: gazed in amazement at the walls and ceiling, peered as they sought their places behind the ornate music stands, and, having taken their seats, looked sceptically across to the choir stalls where sat the dignitaries of the Roman Church. To their eyes the purples and scarlets of these princes of the Church made a fine splash of color. One or two of the younger musicians, too timid to pluck hard at their violin strings, gave diffident coughs. Luise Hammerschmied sat at the harpsichord, her back to the row of bish-

ops and prelates; her hands were in her lap and she was rubbing
them gently together. Without turning her head, her eyes
sought her father who was sitting among the tenors in the middle of the grouped choir. Hammerschmied's eyes were closed
beneath their overhanging brows. His breathing was uneasy,
and his feelings were those the spy must feel who has succeeded
in penetrating right to the head of the enemy's government,
to the very dining table of its president.

Then Pope Gregory appeared dressed in white. With firm
quick tread he walked toward the row of those in scarlet, making
for his splendid seat. All, even the musicians, rose. The Holy
Father stopped beside a small, thickset Cardinal, exchanged two
or three words. Then he sat down, crossed his hands on his
knees, and bowed his head slightly, so that his eyes were no
longer on those present.

The tension went out of the atmosphere. The Cardinals,
prelates, and musicians resumed their seats. The wooden, in-
sensitive expression disappeared from the faces of the visitors,
making way for a cheerful smile round their mouths and eyes.
The voices of the instruments, so far restrained, also rose and
filled the air for so long that impatience and childish inquisi-
tiveness appeared on the faces of the Cardinals, bishops, and
prelates.

The confused, searching voices of the instruments fell silent;
there came the solemn hush before the trumpets ring out.
Luise Hammerschmied let her gaze come slowly back from her
father's head to the music in front of her, and looked at the
right-hand page, to the place where she must come in.

The conductor raised both hands, then he let one drop—
and there was a jubilant outburst of trumpets, clear and fresh,
abrupt and sudden, of violins, drums, and cellos, more familiar

with splendid surroundings, of the voices of the whole choir as they all began singing the omnipotence of the Lord . . .

Magnificat anima mea Dominum! the choir sang. Till then the Catholics had not known what the Lutherans were going to perform. It was Bach's *Magnificat*: a present for the Pope.

Gregory nodded. There was a pleased smile round his mouth. He closed his eyes in obvious delight, the action sending a brief quiver across his thin cheeks. Then he opened his eyes again and looked at the musicians from whom all these cries of joy had come. And from then on his head was never at rest. Eyes and ears were turned from one group to the other; his head beat time with that of a singer which he saw moving rhythmically; it dropped lower when the music became quiet and delicate and reminded them that its subject was the Lord to whom the soul surrendered itself . . . the Lord, who was in each note, each trumpet trill and bell sound of the harpsichord. And in the music, too, was the company of the prophets which Saul met at the foot of the hill of God, coming down from the high place with psaltery, tabret, pipe, and harp before them. And they prophesied. Then the Spirit of the Lord came upon Saul, and he became a different man . . .

When the *Magnificat* was at an end, the musicians gathered round the Pope, clustering in a semicircle. He spoke to them beneath the vaulted, echoing corridors. He was enthusiastic. His voice rang firmly beneath the flat arch, and what he said was an interpretation of the phenomena of their art so simple and comprehensible that the musicians felt they had long been searching for just that formulation without ever finding it.

But did all of them understand him? Even those in crimson and purple?

All do not need to understand the doctrine, Hammerschmied

told himself, standing at the back of the singers. Even the
Lord's disciples who wrote down what He said did not always understand Him. Like the parable in which a grain of
mustard seed is compared to the kingdom of heaven—how
could they have understood that? The expression involved per-
ception of things on which later centuries, a whole two thousand years, were still experimenting. But what did they know
of physics in those days? And what did these know of music?

So, when the Pope called Bach the Fifth Evangelist, it was a
daring expression to use, even though it flattered the clerics,
because they had no sense for the diverse niceties of his mind.
What was the real significance—thus the Bishop of Hamburg
understood it—of the possibility that after the gospel of St.
John there could be one further final interpretation of the
Mysteries, an interpretation which went even beyond the
"pneumatic". . . ?

Then Gregory spoke to individuals. The women seemed to
find it impossible to curtsy and kiss the man's ring, as was
customary. They stood rather shyly. Even Luise. Hammerschmied saw it and was gratified: he stood at the back, half
concealed by the men and women of the choir, keeping in the
background, gladly though he would have spoken with Gregory
and made himself known to him.

Then, suddenly, one of the Cardinals stepped forward:
Platoni. He raised his hand slightly, drawing the attention of
them all, even of Gregory. His lips closed, then opened again,
and he said: "Dear guests from Germany . . . since you have
begun the series of concerts you are to give in many countries,
in this sacred place, I would not wish to neglect recommending
to you and the orchestra, whose instruments, as you will be the
first to agree, are no mere dead objects, the blessing of the
Holy Father."

He stopped as abruptly as he had begun and stepped back again.

One and all, the guests looked at Gregory. Some almost gave their Bishop away with the helpless looks they directed at him in their first alarm. Then, when everybody's eyes were fixed upon him, the Pope said, with a friendly smile that begged their forgiveness, "So be it . . ."

And he gave them his blessing, which after all was not his but that of the Power which he invoked in the formula of the Trinity. Which was exactly what the musicians had just done in singing the final, jubilant *Sicut erat in principio et nunc et semper . . .*

CHAPTER 5

Anxiety swept through the ranks of Gregory's opponents and friends when in the following winter he suddenly became ill and took to his bed. Was this the end? The Pope was seventy-four. He had never been ill before; no one could remember that happening, not even he.

Morning, though still only twilight, was gleaming into the Pope's room. Outside, the sun had not yet reached above the Vatican roofs into the garden. Slowly the dome of St. Peter's acquired a delicate brightness. The edge of the shadows sank to the bowl of the square below the somewhat theatrical steps of the cathedral; the brightness brushed down the bronze-tinted columns of the colonnade. Long shadows ran across the stones, and half the great square with its black obelisk became plunged in the warm fire of the sun; in it the silvery fountains were like plumes in the morning wind that kept them bent to the west. On the far and near sides of the Tiber, the woods on the hills were beginning to quiver, dew was falling, and the mist disappearing in the deep bed of the river. While this exquisite time of genesis continued, the modest world of the Eternal City lay in perfect brightness.

It was a winter's morning in Rome, though it did not deserve the name, for the fruits of autumn were still in the gardens.

Gregory was aware of all this, as he awoke that morning in the twilight of his room after a troubled sleep. Whether you were organist in Burgundy, abbot, or Pope, waking up always followed the same rules, the guardian angels remained the same. Encompassed in the confined world of sleep, which had produced unfamiliar pictures in dreams, and still intent on forgetting all that lay on the far side of sleep, you temporarily revived, became a person awakening, and fed on this oblivion: ageless, you clutched at the very first thought, until sudden recollection of place and time dealt you the first blow. Then you wished you were back asleep, or you longed to get up in order to dispel the shadow of reality in action and deed.

It was Gregory's habit, as it had been in the monastery, to wake some time before the signal which was meant to rouse him. The Sisters always found him lively when they came. The half hour which he gained thereby belonged to him alone. Rome awaited him beneath his windows. The roar was not that of the sea nor of the forest with its wild torrent in that valley in Burgundy, but that of the city at the foot of the palaces: the fountains, the wagons crossing the square of St. Peter on their way from the Tiber, slanting through the columns of the colonnades into the web of alleyways of Trastevere.

In the bright, lavish light of morning Gregory usually reached out for a book and read. Latterly it had been St. Bernard's works that he kept beside him; and it was that great, strong saint who was the subject of the paper that Gregory was writing in those early hours. Nor was he intending to do anything but that on this particular morning.

There were evil tongues which asserted that his faith was

weak. He had now been Pope seven years, yet during his reign there had not been one event of importance to which you could point as redounding to his glory or that of the Church. He had proclaimed no new dogma, had not even once canonized, and all the proceedings were coming to a stop. He was even known to have said: "Produce a real saint and I will confirm him." Was he waiting for a new St. Bernard to be brought to him?

At any rate, he had once said: "A sacred awe comes over Us when We remember the history of the West and how in the Middle Ages it culminated in such figures of faith as Saint Bernard."

So one day the theologians asked themselves whether history did not still have hidden away a figure or two to equal the great saints. They investigated, found and put strange names before the Pope. The resources of the Middle Ages had not yet been exhausted. Reports on many Bernards were brought to the Pope, merely to procure their feasts for the Church under Gregory. He, however, perceived this and waved them aside. Did he have something better in mind?

That night his sleep had been uneasy and black. He longed to be at work, and for that alertness of mind which work always brought him. But as he raised his head and looked at the light, it felt as heavy as it might have felt after a drinking bout. A slight giddiness made his head swim. He groped for his spectacles and put them on. The light was like milk welling through the curtained window. Reality had come trespassing into his dreams that night. His eyes had seen evil pictures, wildly confounded and senselessly mixed. And one and all had corresponded with Gregory's reality, with his day, with the things he was accustomed to hear from his advisers.

Of course he did not believe in interpretation of dreams,

yet he took it as a warning that in one of those dreams no other than Hopkins had reproached him with not having yet given the faithful a new saint.

Gregory sat up. How gladly would he have given them a new saint. They might regard him as weak in faith . . . he himself felt strong. It was in regard to people that he felt weak. They were not so easy to get at. But as concerns God he had always felt himself strong. It is true that his faith was simple, as was demanded of the monk in his cell: his relationship to Heaven was strong and clear. He prayed to God, as the Athenians were once bidden to pray to their deity: "O God, give rain."

He closed his hands, intertwined his fingers, squeezed them together, and in calling the name of the Lord called himself fully awake: "God, come swiftly to my help."

And: "O God, make a new saint manifest to your Church, so that I can nominate him."

Then he wanted to greet the day; he got up, slipped into his leather slippers which had fur inside, into his dressing gown, and hurried to the window. He jerked the curtain aside by the long heavy-tasseled cords. That called forth a long-drawn-out sound which, as the light burst in, brought after it all the noise and bustle of St. Peter's Square.

Gregory laid hold of the window fastening, tugged at it in order to open the right-hand side which itself was taller than a man. Then, all at once, he was aware of a weakness in his hand. He set his left hand on top of his right and pulled with both together. They grew still weaker, he rubbed them together and finally banged one with the knuckles of the other. His head was clear again after that initial attack of giddiness, yet now his knees were reeling, his feet failing him. He had not the strength to take a step. He clutched across at the edge

of the bed, propped himself up with both arms, and let his
body slowly fall.

"I'm ill," Gregory thought. "Perhaps my strength will return
if I allow myself another half hour's sleep. I will have to say
Mass a little later. O God, give me a little more sleep."

His strength did not return. When the nuns entered the
room they found the Pope halfway between waking and sleep-
ing. His forehead was pale, his lids half closed; his cheeks had
more folds than usual, his lips were dry and cracked and craving
moisture.

Pope Gregory was ill.

The Vatican became very quiet. The dignitaries stopped
when they met and asked each other how the Pope was. All
of a sudden there was anxiety in every face. Christmas was
near. They prepared to celebrate it without the Holy Father.
Gregory would have to be in bed a long time. White and
limp, his hands lay motionless beside each other on the linen
sheet. He had not the strength to fold them. The doctors,
the Sisters, and two men had access to his sickroom. Cardinal
Secretary of State Hopkins made the Pope a daily report. Part
of the business was handed over to Cardinal Platoni, and he
too came frequently, stood waiting and looking with anxious
expression at the scarcely perceptible figure beneath the sheet,
shaking his head if Gregory lay sunk in sleep, and going away
to return when he was awake. Then he said nice kind things to
him, which had a tender ring that was unwonted coming from
him. The Pope's affliction grieved him.

"The anxiety of a new election weighs heavily upon us," he
admitted once to inquiring passers-by. "It's eight years since
we elected Gregory and fetched him from his monastery. We
have often thought hard things of his wilfulness; yet it was an
almost miraculous solution when our choice fell on the French

abbot. We cannot say that his rule has not proved a blessing to the Church and to the world. We have been granted years of peace. God grant that he recovers. For the question of whom to choose which caused us such difficulties eight years ago is no easier today."

Platoni had every cause for anxiety. Gregory had made himself friends among the younger, newer Cardinals, whom he himself had appointed. So far no one had tried to assess how the forces were divided. And it was quite possible that, if the Pope died, Hopkins would be chosen as his successor. Platoni himself entertained no thoughts of the possibility of his own election. He felt that he was neither called nor qualified to take the helm. Also he was already very old; Hopkins on the other hand he considered too young. He himself had never wanted to do more than just his bit, the one thing that he knew he could do, which was to keep the Church on the line which was there to be read in her own history.

One morning Platoni met Hopkins near the papal rooms. The one was as anxious and distressed as the other. They recognized that. Hopkins spoke to Platoni and asked his advice. Platoni felt that this was the moment to try to win Hopkins to his ideas. He succeeded. First, they were to hold a joint service and entreat the Trinity for the Pope's recovery. Platoni celebrated, Hopkins assisted. Hopkins agreed with the Italian that once Gregory was well on the way to recovery they must do everything to try to induce him to take that step which would bring joy to the community of the faithful. Meanwhile they waited.

Gregory himself believed that with January his strength would begin to return. Christmas was past, the New Year was being celebrated; cold came; snow fell in Rome, thawed; cold weather persisted, milder days followed. Slowly the Pope re-

covered the mastery of his pale hands; the backs of them
regained their light brownish shimmer; the patches on the
skin disappeared. And one day he asked for a book to read, and
again occupied himself with St. Bernard.

With that, Cardinals Platoni and Hopkins felt that the time
had come to lay their joint request before the Pope. They went
to him. The elder left the talking to the younger man. "We
know," said Hopkins, "that in a short time your health will
be as good as ever, indeed that your recovery will give you a
new lease on life. Nonetheless, at this moment, on the boundary
between death and life, we venture to submit to Your Holiness that any day the Lord may require the services of his
earthly representative for heaven itself, so that we will have
him no more. Will not our Holy Father communicate to us
all his powers, will you not establish a feast day, help to hasten
and complete the canonization proceedings, so that they may
commemorate Your Holiness and at the same time impress
the world of the faithful? None in all our Church doubts that
in our Holy Father we have been given a man who has been
entrusted with the powers of the angels. See how all our eyes
are upon you, expectant!"

Gregory looked up with a smile and nodded.

"Have courage, my children, the Lord will not have given
me back my strength for nothing. Therefore I will at once try
to do what is expected of me—as far as lies in my power."

The eyes of the two Cardinals filled with joy and gratitude.
They bowed in admiration and left the room. Outside they
shook hands in silence and walked off, relieved, in the same
direction.

On the very day that spring began, Gregory's health was
fully restored. The hills of Rome and the gardens of the
countryside outside the walls were fragrant with the first blos-

soms of March as the Pope got up from his bed, supported by
Sisters Clara and Raphaela. Day after day, night after night, all
the time he lay in bed, the two had remained at their post
before his door, or even at the foot of his bed, rosaries twined
round their hands.

Now they helped Gregory into his splendid robes. There he
stood, dressed in white; still a little unsteady on his legs, yet
upright; with cheeks pale and hair perfectly white, for it had
lost the color of the melting snows and was as silvery as moon-
lit cloud over a nocturnal sea. It was scarcely distinguishable
from the little cap that he once more wore on his crown. When
the two Sisters saw in what direction the Holy Father's wishes
lay, they left the room, a simple satisfied smile on their lips.
Outside they squatted down on two stools by the door and
smoothed their long robes with small, red, devotees' hands.

"Is he really going to play?" they asked each other.

It was a long time since Gregory had tugged at that window
catch and collapsed. Now, with hands grown strong again, he
held the case within which his violin lay in its velvet. He
wanted to have it in his hands, to play on it, even before he
went to the window to look at Rome, alive and resplendent in
the spring sunlight, whose familiar features he had not seen
for three whole months. He freed it, that perfect shape, from
its crude case that was like a dull negative of a violin. He
heard it sound in his hands before he had even touched the
strings. Then he took his bow, made it taut with its crystal tip,
tuned the strings like a boy avid for music, and struck up,
firm and precise. Up and up rose the gradation of a Bach
chaconne. Step by step the miraculous order of the music
recapitulated the miracle of his recovery. Steeply rose the line
of the piece, confidently detached itself from the earth, and
climbed up and beyond the solitary figure who held the instru-

ment in his hand and seemed to grow smaller and smaller beneath the greatness of the music. It was an immaterial Jacob's
ladder this, as, stage by stage, the steps of the chaconne
mounted.

Wonderful were the thoughts of that old man.

The music died away. The violin slid from Gregory's hand,
once more just an empty shell deserted by its miraculous in-
habitants, and, the music that had issued from it now a sec-
ondary thing. There he stood with empty hands, his head
tilted slightly, as he listened in the ensuing stillness, at that
point where the scene of ascension is abruptly divested of God,
and he told himself what amounted to the following:

That he was attempting too much when he sought to ac-
company the miracle into those giddy heights. For, in spite
of everything, humility was the only thing. No saint—so he
admitted to himself—could ever be like Christ, no musician
like Bach. One must remain modest. But if only once, just
once, in all his humility, he could shout out his joy and proclaim to all humanity the daring concept of the creative order
of the world. If, just once, he could force all who should
hear it, force everybody to their knees before art, before sacred,
awe-inspiring art, as being the purest demonstration of the
divine power and of the heavenly existence.

Pope Gregory dreamed on, dreamed the daring dreams of
the boy whom music has singed with its fire like the first experience of love, yet with greater force and with no fear of
suffering and disappointment. But he was no boy. He was an
old man. And he was not only an old man. He was the Pope.
Elected by fifty-nine Cardinals in all but miraculous circumstances.

And a Pope's ideas, so Gregory told himself, were not so
much dreams as realities. Yes—how he could reveal this dream

of his, this idea of Saint Jean-Sébastien. And it was so easy, so simple: and then it would be reality.

Outside was the daylight. Gregory went to the window and looked down into the garden. Could he risk going out, dared he? He must take care of himself, if he were to realize his dream, were to put his idea into effect. . . . The sky was radiantly blue, and yet the air was chill in the shadows. It was springtime; snow still glistened on the near-by mountains, covering their tops like frayed caps, but the gardens were green. Gregory called; the Sisters appeared and enveloped him in a white cloak. He wanted to walk in the sun.

It was the first day of spring, and also, Gregory remembered, Johann Sebastian Bach's birthday.

CHAPTER 6

A̲FTER E̲ASTER Bishop Hammerschmied received a second letter from the Pope. Unlike the first, this had an official character, although it, too, was written in the Pope's own hand. The Bishop deferred replying. His family, remembering his previous excitement, missed the delight he had shown on that occasion and waited in vain for him to answer the letter. Instead he wrote to the Bishop of Lower Saxony. Then, after the two had talked together on the telephone, Hammerschmied even drove to Hanover to consult with his friend. Bishop Linnich suggested that they summon their fellow bishops.

The Bishop of Hamburg's invitation to Wiebrechtshausen was accepted by the Bishops of Hanover, of Oldenburg, of Saxony, of Weimar, by the Bishops of Stuttgart, Munich, and Lübeck, by the Bishop of Copenhagen, by a bishop from Finland, and by one or two others from neighboring countries.

Grave and serious, Hammerschmied stood back from the French windows which led onto the terrace at Wiebrechtshausen, watching the cars driving into the courtyard. In front of him on the table lay the letter from Rome. He was going to read it out straightway, at their first meeting, which was being held in the old refectory. Those who had not already come the evening before were now arriving in the courtyard. Many came in their own cars, others with the bus which stopped at the gate on the Northeim–Seesen road.

Wiebrechtshausen is a former monastery estate situated at the foot of the Harz Mountains. It lies in a dog-leg bend between low hills and mountains, among fields and woods, at the point where the plain gives place to the first of the hills and valleys. It is medieval in character; the old layout has been preserved intact. The gateway lies in the shadow of aged chestnut trees; the courtyard bears traces of the cattle whose sheds are on the far side of it; dogs and poultry run about it. There is paving along the side of the buildings. Wooden stands for milk churns faded by the weather, polished and scored with use, stand there firmly embedded in the ground. And to the right, behind the gateway entrance, you pass the arched, seldom-used portal of a Romanesque church. This is tiny, consisting of just a nave; the vestry which you enter from the rear across the grass path of the kitchen garden shows Gothic additions and improvements. There is no tower; the roof does not even carry a crossbeam with a bell. The gables of the dwelling houses are old and stepped; the roofs of the buildings, the barns, and the sheds are thatched with straw and reach almost to the ground. Apart from the house and the church all the buildings are of wood.

The Lutheran bishops came to this place, which none of them knew, as to a family gathering. Eventually they were all seated facing each other in what had once been the refectory. Hammerschmied entered with the Pope's letter in his hand. They looked at him expectantly, for it was obviously he who was going to explain their invitation, since Linnich, who had signed it with him, had all the time been sitting silent in his place. He had evaded all questions; yet, unlike Hammer-schmied, he was taking the business lightly and gaily. He enjoyed being able to keep the suspense alive, and so refused to say anything. Hammerschmied, on the other hand, was feeling the gravity of the occasion. It was, after all, his situation; already they were calling him Gregory's friend.

He welcomed the company, laid the letter before him on the long refectory table, at which once the monks had sat, moved it this way and that with both hands until it was at right angles to the edge of the table, and said:

"My dear colleagues! I took the advice which Brother Linnich gave me after I had received a second letter from Pope Gregory, and invited you to come and be my guests. And so that both you and I should be perfectly free, and in order to avoid the semblance of constraint from an official setting, I asked you to come here to this estate, which, though once, it is true, a monastery, has now for close on five hundred years been in the possession of my family."

Then the Bishop looked down at the floor and went on more slowly: "I would like now to read out to you Gregory's letter. Please believe that it is his second. In saying that let me dispel the rumors that represent me as carrying on a regular correspondence with the Pope."

The Bishop of Hanover, who already knew the contents, looked up, eyebrows raised, and saw the attentive, intent faces of the others. Then the Bishop of Hamburg read Gregory's letter.

"Dear Brother," wrote the Pope, "We are sending Our letter to you again, are speaking to you although this time We wish to address the largest possible number from among you. By God's loving will recovered from Our illness, We are again over-

burdened with work and thoughts. These burdens We gladly
bear, and We still find time enough to give free play to idle
dreams and wishes. We feel strong in the health that has been
restored to Us and would gladly employ this freedom to give
joy to all and Ourselves to receive it. For a long time now We
have been pursuing a special idea and would gladly see it
become reality. May the moment in which We write to you
for the second time prove a good beginning. We still owe you a
debt of gratitude for the visit of your musicians who, now a
long time since, gave Us here in Rome of their divine talent.
We have been considering what outcome there could be, and
in the end no other plan can find favor with Us than the
following one, which is closely allied to Our own sentiments
and ideas. Where art is uncontaminated, innocent of vulgarity
and all too human influences, it is closely linked with belief,
bears the marks of belief, itself impresses fresh marks, is even
capable of awakening belief.

"We invite you, ask you to come and spend some days with
Us. But, dear brother, We would like to be able to greet not
just you alone; it would greatly add to Our pleasure if you
and We could manage to get your friends and colleagues, the
representatives of your church, to come to Rome with you, in
so far as they have the desire and inclination for talks together, for a joint festival which shall be dedicated to Johann
Sebastian Bach. We suggest that our days be spent not in
Rome itself, but in Our summer residence, Castel Gandolfo.
It should be possible, I would think, for you and Us to meet
in the spirit of Bach without tempers being aroused too
much . . ."

That concluded the text of the letter. The Bishop, himself
aware of a rush of emotion, raised his eyes from the sheet of

paper and looked into the unmoved faces of his friends. Most held their heads low.

At last they began to look up, gazed round them, and shook their heads. Throats were cleared one after the other. Some were smiling amusedly or even ironically. The first to express an opinion was the Bishop of Lübeck. "I take it," he said, "that none of us will go, not even Brother Hammerschmied. Otherwise he would not have told us of it so dispassionately."

"But he wasn't telling us of his own will!" cried the Bishop of Oldenburg aggressively. "He simply had to inform us of this. He couldn't have done anything else! The letter may be addressed only to him, but it is meant for us all!"

Hammerschmied raised his hand. "I have asked you here so that we can take counsel together whether or not we should accept the invitation in the spirit in which it is intended. There is one other possibility, that I alone should go, and that I take my cantata singers with me again."

The Bishop of Dresden said that he thought the Pope's invitation was too clear for them to take it that way. They were faced with a clear-cut decision, either to accept or to decline. There were no intermediate solutions.

"Then we'll accept!" cried the Bishop of Oldenburg.

"Impossible."

Voices became loud and excited. It was impossible, they declared flatly. They must refuse.

Then in a voice that drowned all the others, the Bishop of Oldenburg cried: "Why can't we? Because it's the Pope? Suppose it was from the Caliph of Tetuan! My dear brothers, please, we daren't, we can't refuse. We can't, if only because it would offend against every commandment, against tact and politeness. Here we must simply do—what we have long since forgotten—and that is adhere to what Our Lord Jesus Christ said: 'Open unto him that knocketh.' And it is just at our door, at our hearts, at the door of the chamber of our hearts, that Gregory has knocked. And we must open it!"

"I would ask you just to consider," said the Finn calmly, "whether the Pope would have come if we had invited him, let us say, to a World Church Day in Stockholm . . ."

Again the Bishop of Oldenburg jumped up; but instead it was the Bishop of Hamburg who spoke. "There is a difference," he said, "between us inviting the Pope and him us. And then we have not invited him. We would never have had grounds to invite him, not even to think of doing so. But he has dared to do it. For it certainly took daring. We know that the Pope has exposed himself to dangers and difficulties with the mere invitation; as he himself suggests in his letter, I mean where he drops into the 'I' form and writes that it is a question of not arousing tempers too much. I read the letter out to you, knowing that we would not be able to agree in the first quarter of an hour. Let us now be patient and wait until each of us has considered it at leisure. Have a look round the house and the farm, and leave your decision till we forgather this evening in the little chapel. That, by the way, is a gem, and its organ is one of the oldest in the country."

They dispersed. Beneath the freshly leaved trees in the garden, some of which were thick with blossom, round the tables on the terrace, on the field and woodland paths outside the precincts, groups formed round the two or three who had definite views. The Bishop of Hamburg gathered a little circle round him, as did the Bishops of Oldenburg and Lübeck. Others however, could not—or could not yet—bring themselves to listen to the arguments of the others. It was a fine, bright day. They walked through the woods and thought they would await the outcome of the discussion, no matter which way it went.

The talks went on throughout the forenoon, were silenced at table, and continued in the afternoon. In the evening they all met in the little church. The sun shone in almost horizontally through the open portal. Bishop Hammerschmied played them in on the silver-toned organ, with a piece of Bach's —and that acted as a starting point for the discussion, when they again sat at table in the hall. In the meantime the excitement had died down, and the objections put forward against accepting the papal invitation were ones of substance.

"What is it he really wants?" they asked. "Is he planning a reunion? Are we to be the ones on whom he's going to try out the idea?"

"Or is it an attempt to take possession of Bach, the Lutherans' Bach? Is he wanting to make Bach a Catholic?"

Soothingly the Bishop of Hamburg put in: "We can scarcely assume that Gregory is plotting to surprise us with anything questionable. Besides, Bach has long been played in the Vatican and in many Catholic churches. I have heard him in St. Peter's, and I have myself had him performed in the Sistine Chapel, and Gregory was in the audience. To what extent Bach himself professed allegiance to the old Church can be gathered from his works . . ."

There was no end to the argument; many no longer understood why so much fuss was being made; any who wanted were at liberty to perform him when and where they pleased.

"Brothers," said Hammerschmied finally, "would it not be a good thing to continue this discussion with Pope Gregory, who after all is not only the Pope, but also one of the most eminent Bach experts of our time? And why should we not at the same time listen to what else he, as Pope, has to say about it. I suggest then that we accept the Pope's invitation and choose the right people from among us for these talks in Castel Gandolfo."

"I concur," said the Bishop of Oldenburg, speaking first.

"I, too, concur," said the Bishop of Hanover.

The spell was broken. Most of them agreed with the suggestion, and the Bishop of Hanover said: "The number of those in agreement is great enough for us to decide to do it."

Very soon the public heard of the conference, and of its object. The Lutheran bishops, so people learned to their surprise, joy, or indignation, had accepted an invitation from Pope Gregory and were going to Rome to spend some days with him in the spirit of Johann Sebastian Bach. They were to go that June. They would play music and discuss the significance of works of art. Many voices were raised against this. And those whose own concurrence had cost them such a struggle now found themselves having to defend their attitude. Yet the controversy soon aroused in many a flickering flame of enthusiasm for the imminent festival in the south, whose subject was to be the musical evangelist of the north.

CHAPTER 7

SUMMER IN ROME. Even the early morning was full of warmth and insects; the sun swung up vigorously over the mountains and shone down into the awakening streets. The open windows of the houses were gleaming golden, and in the shade markets were being held. A hum arose like that of a hive, becoming a roar like that of surf: lorries coming from the main market place, little tricycle carts and motor bicycles, their sidecars piled high. All Rome seemed motorized. Voices and singing; trams rolled along, buses drove up softly and stopped abruptly, and the dammed-up pedestrian traffic thrust past their man-high radiators. Banks and exchanges opened glass doors; ventilator fans whirred, superior people passed through marble pillars with gold-lettered name plates into the halls of the god who has outlived all other heathen gods. Mercury was the only god still mentioned by name in the world of public commerce. But at the same time it was Christian Rome, the Rome of the Pope, of a thousand churches and saints; and there were name plates showing that even banks named themselves after the Santo Spirito. And the young girls who rode in trams and buses to their work carried in their purses medallions on which the

Madonna was stamped, hoping that she would be their patroness and help to increase their cash.

Midday brought stillness to the Eternal City. The rattle of motors decreased; the guttural cries of those who sold fruits and fruit juices, carrying their trays on their heads through the streets of Trastevere or in the neighborhood of the Piazza di Spagna, fell silent and the wind became audible, rustling in plane trees, cypresses, and palms. Somewhere or other each hawker would have sat himself down in the shade of a house, or at a table in an inn to have his meal of bread and wine with something cooked by his wife, his daughter or mother, and kept warm in a can which the innkeeper had let him put under the counter in the early morning. And he would have found companions, men from the workshops of the neighborhood who were having their meal like him.

There would be talk as they ate and drank, their hands scarcely wiped clean of oil and carpenter's glue. They would speak of the summer, of the fountains of Rome and their water which you mixed with your wine, and which was cool even in summer. Sport, films, politics, and the Holy Father were their topics. The latest from the Vatican, read in the newspapers, would be recounted for the hundredth time and listened to with the patience of simple people, pious and naive and yet excited. All current canonization proceedings were to be concluded. At Christmas the Pope was going to canonize a nineteenth-century Pope, and a nun who had written books and, some years before, during the Second World War, suffered a martyr's death in Germany. Nonetheless Platoni and the other theologians had to swallow a bitter pill. After his recovery, Gregory had gone to work with a zeal that was remarkable. Till then no one had seen him zealous. Latterly he had even insisted, despite the opposition of all the Cardinals, that the "meat-eaters," the Protestants from Germany, were to come to Castel Gandolfo, his summer residence.

And the question now asked was: "How would they be received in Rome?"

Naturally the Pope's extravagances, as his veiled plans were called, had caused bad blood. Things were said such as "In the spirit of Johann Sebastian Bach—that sounds like: In the spirit of Benedict of Nursia or of Bernard of Clairvaux."

Of course, both Pope Gregory and Johann Sebastian Bach had their friends within the confines of the Vatican. And these said: "Why not!" Yet one day Gregory had to listen to the criticism even of his most devoted friend and secretary, Hopkins.

"It's too unorthodox, Holy Father," said Cardinal Hopkins, and he was very wrought-up. "We are not dealing with musicians whom, of course, one can invite to Rome to spend some days in the Alban Hills with the Holy Father for the latter's relaxation; we are dealing with theologians of the heresy. But that this would-be theology of a mistaken philosophy was not constructed with the inspiration of the Holy Ghost is a conviction not confined to Cardinal Platoni and Monsignore Mancini. It can, perhaps, be regarded as a sort of auxiliary, a necessary result of the apostasy of Luther that cannot now be changed."

"Nonetheless," said Gregory soothingly, "we must thank God for their existence. They have often been good allies in the struggle against the secular enemy."

"I admit that," said Cardinal Hopkins. "Whatever I may feel, I have personal experience of that. But what induced Your Holiness to take this sensational decision is a mystery not only to the other members of the Holy Office but also to me. We have not been able to prevent the impression getting about that the Holy Father is harboring secrets, that Your Holiness is secretly forging plans of which the dignitaries of the apostate church are to be apprised even before any members of the Holy Father's circle is informed of them."

Secretly impressed by the other's vehemence and himself speaking with unwonted vigor, Gregory said: "My dear Hopkins, whom We are dealing with is best known to Us who are venturing to receive the Lutheran bishops. Go on, if you like, pretending to the others that the Pope needs relaxation after his illness. I, however, feel strong and fit and am well on the way to turning one òr two ideas into facts, so that when I leave this world I shall be able to say that I have done my part. But as for apprising Our advisers, to whom We have always given heed, unless Our action were the result of a direct talk with God as is now and again vouchsafed to each miserable one of us—like a quenching shower of rain to the most desolate tract of the Sahara—in order to give the lonely and thirsting strength and courage for the last prayer, We will not inform the Cardinals of these ideas until We consider the time ripe."

Gregory had spoken spiritedly, breathing heavily; several times, even, he had left his seat, folded his hands and unfolded them again. On Hopkins' face was a scared expression. His eyes still hung on the other's mouth when Gregory had long finished, and in them was all the helplessness of the schoolboy who, having gone too far in something hasty he had said, wellfounded though it might be, would now really like to tell the master how utterly abject and squashed he feels. Yet he remains true to himself, because Youth never loses its force; only he wants to employ this youth in a different direction, wants to offer his services to Age.

Cardinal Hopkins bowed his head, seized Gregory's hand, and with closed lips touched the Fisherman's ring. "Forgive me," he said. "I will do my part and continue to defend Your Holiness against all opponents."

His departure after the conclusion of the Easter festivities was official. He boarded the big limousine, whose hood was as high as the bow of a ship and ended in a big silvery grill and four circular headlights tapering parabolically to the rear. Two of the headlights had the usual frosted glass, but two smaller ones which were mounted above and set in from them gave an orange-colored light. Pope Gregory had scarcely ever driven at night. In front, at the steering wheel, sat Ernest, the French chauffeur, and behind him on the leather upholstery sat the Pope in his white. They left the Vatican at noon and drove round the walls of St. Peter's toward the arched gateway that led out into St. Peter's Square. Before they reached it, two motorcyclists joined them. The great machines were like animals, and the two riders astride them looked, in their black leather jackets and crash helmets, like grim, commanding angels, arms wide-spread and curved like bat wings. Two others waited with thundering motors by the side wall of the sacred basilica, where it bends outward by the apse. They brought up the tail of the cavalcade and set off as soon as the Holy Father's black car had passed, riding close together. Beyond the steps of the church the road curved on the far side of the gateway into the bowl of the square. Even before they had left the square and turned into a side street instead of into the cool, sober approach road of Via della Conciliazione, the drivers had begun to put on speed. On the right bank of the Tiber they headed for the Porta Portese, the old exit from the city.

At that hour it was quiet in the little streets. All the churches were shut, the people sitting in the shade. Suddenly those who were still up and about were swept onto the pavement by the appearance of the motorcyclists, clearing the way for the car behind them at the speed, unsuitable for the inner city, of fifty miles an hour. They crossed the Tiber by the Ponte Sub-

licio and so to the Porta di San Paulo, out into the city and on
to the Alban Hills, a clear familiar sight from the streets on the
hills and declivities of the Eternal City. Somnolent beggars,
vendors of fruit juices, flower women, and children looked up
as they heard the familiar noise of the cavalcade. Then they
jumped to their feet, waved, and shouted: *Evviva il Papa!*"

CHAPTER 8

THE CITY WALL with the pine trees of the Protestant cemetery and the evening sky for a background was like a Japanese picture. The glowing colors of the setting sun fell slantingly across the many gardens in the countryside, the horizontal beams no longer illuminating the dense shadows of the walls and treetops. At the end of the day clouds had formed in the monotonous summer sky and hung in a broad fan-shaped corridor leading from the sea across the city to the hills. On them was being performed the miracle of the changing colors.

A suburban train of the Ostia line discharged hundreds of trippers coming from the Lido. Hawkers, grown more active as the heat abated, at once came running up and offered their fruit. Brown faces poured out of the station and ran their eyes across the square, looking for the waiting buses and the trams across by the San Paulo Gate. There were men in green, with yellow leather boots, guns, and fierce dogs four on a leash, returned home from the thickety, marshy coastal area, their frayed canvas bags full of feathered game. Along with them were students, laborers, women, and children, who had been making full use of their Sunday. And from all these the face of a girl detached

itself, deeply browned by the summer. The skin on the forehead and beneath the eyes had reddish speckles from the sun.
The gaze of her brown eyes went roaming across to the tram
which stood waiting at the gate. The girl quickened her pace.
Her hair was fairer than usual that evening; it had been washed
by the sea and fell bushy and wind-plaited onto her shoulders
without trace of a comb. There was still sand from the beach
in it, and on her un-made-up lips was the taste of the salt of
the sea. The girl wore a white summer dress and a little coat
of the same material hung over her shoulders. She might have
been in her middle twenties; in one hand she carried a satchel
with her bathing things, in the other a large book of music on
which in Gothic lettering was printed the name BACH. She
ran across the square, past the gray pyramid of Cestius in the
shadow of the trees of the Protestant cemetery, beneath the
weathered stones of the Porta, and over to the tram. She rode
in it to the inner city. She stood still, little chin well up, lips
closed, the music tightly squeezed under her arm, stood there
without fending off the jostling of those thrusting past, and
looked out at the streets now growing dusky, at the roofs of the
cars, into the open convertibles in which sat women in gay,
light summer dresses and men with white peaked caps. A
Roman Sunday was almost over. All the people with whom
Luise Hammerschmied had sallied forth that morning were now
returning to their homes in dense crowds. She alighted at the
Tiber and, without looking right or left, ran up the street to
the Aventine hill. She lived in the heart of a residential district,
in an old house above San Alessio and Santa Sabina, and from
her windows there she could look across gardens and the river
at the calm white dome of St. Peter's.

Her room was in the owner's flat. She climbed the dark stairs,
scaring some cats, opened the door of the flat, walked in and

past the dining room; as her hosts were saying grace she did not greet them. She opened the door of her room and stood face to face with her father. He had opened the window, pushed the folding shutters aside, and had been looking out over the roofs.

"Excuse me," he said. "Your people brought me here."

"Daddy!"

She shook her head, smiling as she did so, and placed the satchel with her bathing things on the washstand, the music on a smaller table on which were papers and sheets of music. Underneath, on the crossbar of the legs, lay a violin in a brown canvas case.

"How long have you been in Rome?" she asked.

"We arrived yesterday evening." Gradually Hammerschmied's voice grew strong and warm. "Your mother, your brothers and sisters, Hamburg, and the whole Cantata Society send their love or kindest regards."

"Has the Society come with you?"

She pushed a chair across for her father, a wooden chair with plaited hempen seat. He sat down. Luise remained standing.

"I haven't much to offer you." Her voice had a dry ring; it was quite saturated with the sun of the Lido. "Some leftover milk, vermouth, a cherry or two, and white bread. Just remains. And you must forgive me for writing so little lately. Letters are as dear as bread."

She shrugged her shoulders, raising her sunburned arms and letting them drop again. As she did so she smiled.

"I understand, Luise," said her father. "How do you like being in Rome?"

He reached out for her hand.

"I like being here very much. I've just come straight from the sea. I went off this morning with the entire population. Four

times I have had to open my mouth: twice in the tram, once at
the window of the ticket office, once to a fruit seller on the
beach. But now you must tell me what brings you to Rome. And
about Hamburg. And the Cantata Society. So you have not
brought them with you?"

"No. But it is still Johann Sebastian Bach who brings us here
again."

"You're not alone?"

Then he told her everything. And when he came to the end of
his tale, Luise said: "Yes, Pope Gregory. If we didn't have him,
Rome would be like any other city in the world."

"And Hamburg?" her father asked.

"Pope Gregory," Luise went on, looking past her father, "is
one of the few men, in fact the only one, who knows what is
wrong with this world. This world, whose days one could almost
wish were numbered. And you asked me about Hamburg! I
would gladly be with you all again . . ."

"Do you need money?"

"A little. I often feed from beggars' bowls, in the students'
mensa, in the nunneries. Don't I live in a lovely place here?
In the midst of so many sacred names. There are San Alessio,
Santa Sabina, and the convents of several orders. Down below,
within reach for Mass each morning, is Maria in Cosmedin,
where we were together that time . . ."

"You said to me then that you could never leave Hamburg,
the Cantata Society. And now Rome has become your home,"
said Hammerschmied in a pained voice. "You may believe it
or not, I found it hard to accept the Pope's invitation and come
to Rome because of knowing you were here. I was acting
against my own feelings, though with complete mental conviction, when I persuaded the bishops in Wiebrechtshausen to
accept the invitation from the Pope."

Luise said: "It must be a lovely summer in Wiebrechtshausen now."

"Come back," her father asked.

"Perhaps," she replied.

Then silence reigned for a while.

Suddenly Luise started out of her thoughts and asked: "What actually does the Pope want of you?"

She spoke thoughtfully and added hesitantly: "I almost believe I know."

"What is it that you know?" asked the Bishop.

"I can't say it," Luise replied. "It would sound strange, crazy even . . ."

After some hesitation her father nerved himself to ask: "Will you ever decide to become a Catholic?"

"No," Luise answered, astonished. She shook her head and caught at her hair that the sea had entwined so softly. "No, I don't think so. At least it has not yet entered my mind, although I very often go down to Santa Maria in Cosmedin to hear a Low Mass. I find that wonderful. But perhaps it's just nonsense what I was saying and thinking about Pope Gregory. I don't know what he wants of you. I have lots of other things I want to tell you."

Louise Hammerschmied had come to Rome to study the music of the Italian baroque. Shortly after she returned with the Cantata Society from the great journey which had taken them through Spain, France, Belgium, and Holland, through the great cities of Western and Central Europe, she decided that she would go to that city of which she retained the most vivid memories—Rome.

Her father at once told himself that they—Cimarosa, Vivaldi, Pergolesi, Albinoni, and Palestrina—could only be an excuse. His daughter was drawn to Rome by the same thing that took

the Bohemians to Paris, the English to Positano, the blind wor-
shipers of past ages to Greece: the firm ground of what was
basically a picturesque, scurrilous, and exotic world that offered
to those who had been uprooted from their homes an opportunity to indulge in laziness or in their own mental, spiritual,
or corporal vice. In the case of this girl musician and Protestant from north Germany, the attraction was the Catholicism
of Rome and its enjoyment of life that is so inimitably and
fantastically innocent and devout.

Was that it?

The Bishop did not find out on that evening. Luise was
bubbling over with gaiety when, late that evening, she took her
father back to his hotel, which was in the vicinity of the Tiber,
a couple of bends of the river away. It was maintained by a
Catholic order, which had been charged with looking after
Protestant visitors, and which did so with such attentiveness
that whatever the previous experience of their guests—as pilgrims, clergymen, or tourists—this reception put it triumphantly
in the shade. The building was magnificent, of white marble,
with large windows, light vestibules, spacious rooms that had
every comfort, and tasteful ornaments as well as the usual pictures of the Madonna. This was the place to which the waiting
cars had brought the bishops and musicians from Germany that
first evening—following the commotion of their arrival at the
main railway station, when they had been surrounded by re-
porters of the press and radio who would let none of them
through.

First they had stood silent in the reception room of the hotel,
their satchels and instruments in their hands, perplexed and
with uncertain, roving eyes. Several wiped the perspiration from
their brows and listened uneasily to the humming of the fans—
so this was Rome! But as they had not kept track of where they

were going, and in any case did not know their way about the
Eternal City in the dark, they wondered: "Are we in the
Vatican?"

Attentive fathers came hurrying up, in black soutanes, with
vivacious, almost childish faces, rosy and smooth. They laughed,
questioned, and gave information, without the Germans ever
finding the courage to voice their question. These men, friendly,
almost brotherly, attentive in every imaginable way, using pantomime, gesture, and guiding hand, took the visitors to their
rooms and invited them down to supper in half an hour's time.
They ate in a body. As soon as the sisters had set the food on
the table, the monks withdrew and left the Protestant theologians, whom the Holy Father had recommended to their
hospitality, to say their own grace and have their meal. They
were in the hotel of a religious order, that of the Pallottines, in
Via Pettinari, close to the Tiber.

It was in front of this building that Luise took leave of her
father. It was quite dark and close upon midnight. The hotel
shone with light from within and without.

Luise walked back to the Tiber in the light of the street
lamps. The night was so warm that you could have slept on the
seats in the Capitol. Beggars and hawkers squatted against the
walls of the palaces. A forlorn figure, she took up her position
on the edge of the curb. A bus, the last to go that night, stopped
by her very feet. She got in and paid, considerably lighter of
heart because of the money her father had given her a short
while before. She had returned from the sea that evening with
her last few lira.

For her the day was not yet at an end. Now that she was alone
again, the great thoughts came. She returned to where she
lived, happy, completely relaxed and filled with a secret joy. It
was not just her father's visit that had made her heart so full;

the reason for her gladness was rather to be found in the talk they had had together. Yet it was not the bare words that had stuck in her memory: there was an idea that had kept itself hidden from her behind her father's words, an idea of which he had been unaware and which she had merely sensed, but now it was there and would not leave her. As she swept up the steeply sloping street, her head was full of melodies which had laid hold of her the moment she had left her father. It was already late, and the street door was shut. The porter opened to her. She waved her hand in thanks and ran up the dimly lit stairs to the top, hissing the tunes unmelodiously through her teeth, a shrill whistle indicating a flourish of trumpets. To herself she kept repeating the name Bach, dividing it up into its four letters so that it also rendered music, the notes B-A-C-H.

Then, as she stood once more in her room, at the open window beneath which shone the calm lights of the Eternal City, she found words for the thought that had come to her as her father was telling her of the music festival in Castel Gandolfo to which Gregory had invited the Protestants. To herself she said: Saint Johann Sebastian.

Was she right in thinking that that too was the Holy Father's idea?

Greatly stirred, Luise Hammerschmied clasped her hands together. It must be so. Only Gregory could think of such a thing and make reality of it. No one could have thought of it earlier. The moment was a favorable one, the time ripe.

What a familiar ring that solemn and yet simple, almost common, word had: Saint Johann Sebastian. His name was the symbol of water, and it was the water that came first, according to Pindar, the poet of the Greeks; yet one day it too would perish in the final heat emanating from the Word of God, just as once His voice brought the light into being and it shone.

Johann Sebastian—son of the poor musician Ambrosius Bach and his wife Elisabeth Lämmerhirt. Did it not sound like something from an old legend, something long familiar, carved in wood, a votive offering, a passage in the Bible, like the one which once proclaimed that at the end of time the Lord would awaken shepherds . . .

As He who was Himself born in a stable is reborn again and again in the daily Mass, so was the medieval love song revived when Johann Sebastian Bach recast it in the chorale O *Haupt voll Blut und Wunden* which her lips were then humming, and which also appears in the Christmas Oratorio as a lullaby, and as a dirge in the Passion.

Oh, had she, Luise Hammerschmied, really echoed Pope Gregory's thought? Could that be? Were thoughts like the stars that stood above the City of the Seven Hills and shone for all who looked up to them at the same moment, to become imbued with the same ideas?

CHAPTER 9

JOHANN SEBASTIAN BACH: in his music faith has become art. And yet, like all artists, he was just a miner in the mine of the Lord who created heaven and earth. The miner descends into the deep strata of the earth in order to find precious stones; by the sweat of his brow, in unutterable toil he must delve in the gloom, must drill and blast, must loosen stones, pick up, select, discard, to get the one diamond for which he is searching. He frees the gem from its natural bed, brings it, still unrecognizable in its prison of scoria, to the daylight, where slowly and laboriously, washing, swilling, chipping, and cutting, he shapes it till it is perfect. And yet in the end he has only uncovered the law that was inherent in the thing itself when it still slept its sleep in the world of darkness. From it he reads off the forms—those of threefold gold, silver, and diamond—and his work obeys the same law. He holds a piece of the world in his hands, a fragment of Creation. Creation in a prism, in the guise of gold, in the gleam of silver, of a stone, a ring, a goblet. In his hands he holds the manifestation of the Lord: art. For, no differently than the miner and goldsmith, the artist too descends into the well of earth's night, labors, creates, drills,

delves for the hidden stone, for the gold that he takes up to the
light and fashions into its perfect shape. And then he too in
word and picture and notes holds the laws of the world in his
hand. And any can come and read them from him, as from the
prophets, can perceive the purity, the consistency, and the
spirit of creation, in accordance with the laws of which music
is also made. For so once must the Lord and the world have
sung, as we can still hear them when the organ sounds in our
ears.

Johann Sebastian Bach, who was not the first nor the last
musician, held tone compressed in his hand, as the Lord once
did the water which came before all else. In his music creation
has become art.

The men in Castel Gandolfo were taking their music out into
the open, confined though it normally is to rooms, halls, and
churches, through using instruments like the organ; and though
music is able to fashion its own Nature, such as you can imagine
being still extant when the world no longer exists. All but two
days of the festival week that Pope Gregory was giving his
guests were gone. They had heard some of Bach's organ works;
a partita for piano; a solo suite for violoncello; preludes and
fugues played on the harpsichord; trios, and the whole corpus of
works large and small which Bach had led into the realm of
art, as Moses once led the Israelites out of bondage into the
Promised Land. They had heard lectures and recitals, delivered
by the Pope, by the Bishop of Hamburg, or by one of the other
guests whom the Pope had invited: two monks, well-known
musical experts from the world of the religious orders, one of
them also Gregory's confessor, together with the Pope and a
young Venetian Cardinal, held the balance against their Protestant guests. They were all specially chosen and together made

up the little orchestra that assembled once a day to perform secular pieces: four of the Brandenburg concertos and two of the orchestral suites, one of which, the first in C major, was to be played that evening in the open in Castel Gandolfo's park.

The Protestants were dressed in black; the two monks, also in black, sat with them among the violins, first of whom was Pope Gregory. Bishop Hammerschmied was always at the harpsichord and conducted. The young Venetian played the viola. The rest of the Protestants were masters of violins, cellos, double basses, or that instrument of German family music, the flute.

The few voices of Nature were still the only ones to be heard on that summer evening. The walls and trees screened off the the last of the sun's rays. Because of the approaching twilight, candles had been affixed to the music stands, their flames protected from the wind by little shields. Before the voices of the instruments began you could hear the near-by fountains soughing and the birds twittering. The players came by the paths of the park to the enclosure where seats had been arranged. Each was in a good mood. They walked in couples or alone. Those who walked by themselves looked about them as though wanting to take in the shape of the hills once more before darkness fell, and listened to the voices in the cooling air.

The days with Pope Gregory had passed all too swiftly. To him, and the music, they owed the emotional freedom in which they had found their way to each other, owed that serenity and shedding of remembered troubles which it created. The men from Germany realized this, and admitted it to each other. They clapped like students when Pope Gregory appeared, the last to arrive. They too had adopted the custom of those who play in secular orchestras, tapping the wooden part of their bows on their violins each time the Pope played as soloist, as he did once in a Vivaldi concerto and again in Bach's E major Concerto. There still remained Gregory's last recital on the following day. He was going to play the E major Partita for violin. That was to be the finale.

Pope Gregory had elected to hold the evening concerts in the open, not because he held the house chapel—where the organ concertos, choral studies, and pieces for solo instruments had been performed—to be an unsuitable place for the secular pieces based on dances, but because on such evenings they had need of Nature, even though they were as fully divorced from it as from the dance. He put the idea into words, expressing it thus: "Worldly all this is: it came into the world, as Our Lord came into the world, drank wine, and was at one and the same time downcast and happy in this world . . ."

They tuned their instruments, Pope Gregory in front, sitting dressed in white at the center and head of the orchestra, not because he was the Pope, but because he was the first violin, from whom the others took their time.

Then the music started, beginning darkly with the overture that has only a few clear overtones. It moves slowly, rises and falls again, travail-bound, over the waters of existence, over which hovers the creative spirit of God. Now the light of the sun is dully forcing its way through the clouds, out of which rain nevertheless still falls, while in the distance patches of sunlight that lie upon the sea gleam golden and draw nearer. They pale, turn back again, and shine forth in different places, like stars which have strayed a little above the clouds. Dark and light contend. Then the Lord speaks: "Let there be light." No shadow may disobey His command. The worldly is still sacral, the mystical-sacral becomes world.

Pope Gregory and his musicians would have liked to have

the other suite, the great Third; but they lacked the loud instruments for this, which even the Psalmist may not dispense with on the day of rejoicing: the drums and trumpets. No one played them. They chose the smaller, though far longer, suite of many parts, which lacks the piety of the slow air and in which the dances crowd one upon the other, their rhythm changing, it is true, yet remaining within the same continuing law.

The overture begins, filled with airy dance that surmounts all obstacles; like a thing let free, it has left the realm of mysticism. At its end comes the beginning once again. For as it was in the beginning is now and ever shall be. Yet once stated is enough. The heaviness has gone, drowned by the light, and there is a sharp break: full stop. Fresh and joyous begins the next piece, on which the main stress is already laid: rondo, gavotte, gigue, minuet, saraband, allemande, courante. Dance follows dance. By the seashore fishermen and farmers, worldly and undoubting, celebrate their festival, past storms and floods already forgotten. It is Shrove Tuesday and that is portrayed by the soft resignation of a trio. Then spirits rise anew: it is Easter and Whitsun, when they spake with tongues, the miracle that repaired the confusion of Babel. The simplest now speak all the languages of the world: Italians, French, Dutch, and German give each other joyous, united rendezvous. Minuet, courante, saraband . . .

The day was not yet at an end; the evening had one further surprise in store for them. The last note of the suite had died away as the first drops fell from the sky. Unnoticed, a thunderstorm had been gathering in the hills, then slowly dropped to the lower valleys and the lake, and now it fell upon them unsuspecting. They looked into the sky; it was dark, only the candles on the music stands cast their glow a couple of paces across the turf, and from behind fell the gleam of the lights in the house. Trees and bushes towered up blackly; there was no difference between their shade and the night sky; not a star was to be seen. They broke up in haste, each carrying his music and his instrument; the harpsichord was borne off by some of the younger brethren who acted as servants in the house. Gregory too took his violin and strode after the others. One of the monks, the Pope's father confessor, took off his scapular with its hood and threw it over Gregory's white garment. The heavy, sudden downpour lasted only a few minutes, then the rain became light again, the big drops falling loudly from the leaves of the trees.

Half an hour later, when the visitors, the two monks among them, were still sitting chatting, Pope Gregory unexpectedly walked in among them. They fell silent as he appeared. He hesitated, smiled, said they must, please, go on and walked up to join their circle.

Yet he did not attend to what was being said; he stood there among them, indeed, but his gaze was directed at the floor; one hand hung limp, the other he held at his breast where it grasped the chain of his cross. He was thinking, searching for ways of expressing the particular thing he had come to say to these men. Suddenly he looked up and directed a questioning glance at the two monks. They seemed to understand him, gave the hint of a nod that no one caught, and after a tactful pause bade the company good night.

They all knew that the monks had their rules to observe; it was understandable that they should retire.

At Gregory's invitation his guests came and gathered round him; they supposed that he wished to join their conversation, or perhaps begin a new one. And when he raised his hand to show that he wished to speak, they looked at him inquiringly. He had remained standing where he was; now he crossed his hands at his breast and said: "We believe that these days have been fruitful ones for us all . . ."

Then he raised his hand and the ring gleamed in the light that streamed from the many lamps on ceiling and walls. All at once the silence was complete.

The Pope, inwardly excited, again folded his hands on his breast and went on: "Jean-Sébastien Bach was the prerogative that We reserved to Ourselves after Our election to this sacred office. Whether this was the reason why Our strength was not confirmed to the same degree as that of Our predecessors I am not able to say. If, however, this was so, then I would humbly take exception and ask that I should be allowed him nonetheless, as any other of the faithful is allowed his patron, and call him saint."

His guests, who already owed so much to his presence during these days, a presence of which they were sensible at all times, even when he was not actually there, nodded their approbation.

"That makes Us wonder," Pope Gregory went on, "whether your approbation is for Our use of the word saint, as which We have always venerated Jean-Sébastien Bach—or whether it was just a spontaneous approval demonstrating a liking for Our Person, for Our rule which has been so innocuous for you. We can assure you, however, that We wrestled for a long time before We dared take such a step which will cause a general sensation. And We must now admit to you at this late hour, which We hope will not be our last together, that there was a deeper purpose behind these days than just that of celebrating the works of Jean-Sébastien Bach."

The Pope fell silent, but only for a moment, then went on a shade more quickly: "In Jean-Sébastien Bach faith has become music . . ."

Again Gregory paused. All eyes were on him. None present

was older than he. The Bishop of Hamburg was the oldest of
the Germans, but even he was only in his early sixties. And it
was not simply in age that the Pope was their superior at that
moment; they sat there as his audience, as they had so often
done in the last few days. He faced them, motionless, his feet
close together and peeping out from the circle of the hem of
his robe, hands clasped together at his breast. His eyes, magni-
fied by the lenses in his glasses, moved alertly this way and that.
No one yet sensed the pinpoint of his speech. They interpreted
it simply as an anthem, as it were, to crown the recitals and concerts of the week.

"His music is a tremendous source of purity . . ."

Gregory spoke in German with a foreign ring to it, and much
of what he said sounded strange and clumsy. If they had all
understood French, he would certainly have expressed himself in
much more sober fashion and more concisely. As it was, it
sounded slightly mysterious, like deep wood wind.

"From it you can draw the same strength as We receive from
reading the Holy Scriptures. Even his secular pieces, such as
that which we played together this evening, are hymns to the
glory of God and to God's joy. Thus overtures became choral
cantatas . . . But what use are words, dear brethren. There was
another reason why We sent for you. For all that We know
how to express has already been said by others, and it seems
superfluous in face of what Jean-Sébastien has himself said in
his wonderful Pentecostal language . . ."

Once more the Pope broke off. For a brief moment he looked
down at the carpet on the floor, then again raised his eyes and
turned them inquiringly on his audience. It was the final pre-
liminary to that which he had to say to them, to ask of them.

"Also, this last thing," he said, "that We are going to say

now has long since been said and thought by most of those who love the temporal and spiritual phenomenon that Bach is: Saint Jean-Sébastien. That is to say, We are sure that he was a saint, that he is a saint. Bach is to be numbered among the saints."

This time Gregory's pause was due to a momentary breathlessness caused by the emphasis with which he had spoken. None of his audience nodded; no one clapped. Now one and all realized what Pope Gregory's project was. Was there opposition or timid agreement to be seen on their faces? They appeared unmoved.

Gregory began again.

"Since this power is invested in Us, We have decided—after consultation with competent persons of our consistory—that We shall proclaim Jean-Sébastien Bach a saint before the whole world; for We are certain that in the eyes of heaven that has long since been done."

Now Gregory neither stopped nor paused. Word followed word; his voice grew stronger and slowly his smile returned, despite the seriousness of what he was saying.

"And you, who are gathered here round Us, should be able to agree with Us without scruple. We asked you here in order to discuss this with you. We wished first to ask *you*, because you are the select guardians of Bach's art and, through having made his music a component of your liturgy, know best the essence of that music and are qualified to decide. We wished to lean upon your counsel."

Gregory had finished. He opened his hands, slightly spread out his arms, and looked inquiringly at his guests. No one had a word to say. Gregory saw it; he had expected it, sure though he was of success. Still keeping a cheerful face, he began to speak once more, clear and loud, asking his guests to take time and think it over calmly. Tomorrow was the last day. He would then be ready to answer questions, to expand his idea and try to win their assent. That meant much to him and was, he felt, worth asking and praying for.

Then he raised his right hand, said, "*Laudetur Jesus Christus*," turned and went.

CHAPTER 10

THE FOLLOWING DAY began with an organ concert in the chapel. The Lutherans were all there and so was Pope Gregory, who a short while before had said Mass at the altar, which now was stripped. The Venetian Cardinal and the two Benedictine monks were not there, being then about their spiritual duties. The Germans, however, understood it as meaning that the Pope wished to speak with them again. What he had said on the previous evening already lay locked, dreamlike, behind them, and no one yet had found access to it. As soon as the Pope appeared their whispering stopped; they got to their feet and inclined their heads in greeting. Gregory took his place, the Lutherans sat down again, and the Bishop of Hamburg began to play. One organ piece followed the other; little images appeared in sound, delicate pictures spun through the air, variations on pastoral themes and church hymns. Fantasia, quiet, restrained, heartfelt works in which was no ferment. To conclude, Hammerschmied played Bach's last chorale, the melody on the double text: *Wenn wir in höchsten Nöthen sein* and *Vor deinen Thron tret' ich hiemit.*

A smile and a look of comprehension came onto Pope Gregory's face as he heard the first notes. He supposed, of course,
that they must all now feel how necessary was the project he
had put to them. Could there be anything else in the hearts,
or in the heads, of these men who, yesterday evening, had
looked at him so perplexedly, so without comprehension? A
stormy discussion must surely have broken out after he had
left them; certainly their feelings, their minds would still be
agitated by his surprising request. The fact that the Bishop
of Hamburg was now playing this last chorale of Johann
Sebastian's was a little favor, a concession, or so he thought it.
Was not just this a better way of winning the hearts of men
than words?

When the Lord on Golgotha in the hour of His death said,
"It is finished," the heathen centurion beneath the cross was
moved and acknowledged Him to be the Son of God. There
was the same ring about this piece which Bach in the blindness
of old age had dictated to another hand: *Es ist vollbracht—vor
deinen Thron tret' ich hiemit.* He meant: "Now—in this hour
I appear before Thy Throne." And also: "With this, this
work, with all works, all my works, the works of virtue and of
art, I come before Thee." What was not expressed, however,
was this: "Oh, accept it graciously." As far as Bach was concerned, he was sent into the world to express the Creation in
music. Do not say: "God sends no one into the world for
that purpose, for none can accomplish that better than God
has been able to do. What the artist achieves are but aftermaths to the Creation." Not that. Possibly they are preludes,
as the Son too was only a prelude; for God is always sending
into the world those through whom He wishes to make Himself
audible and visible. He sent His own Son, became Himself
man, although certainly He could not repeat Himself on earth

as He was from the beginning. *Et Nunc Et Semper*. So, with this.

If they would decide honestly, these Lutheran bishops and scholars, then they would give their assent. For here it was a question of breaking with all other considerations aimed at the temporal prosperity of their church.

But they had scruples, these Lutherans with Bishop Hammerschmied at their head. Their views were hard and unyielding. Nor did they change them when the concert was over and Gregory left them by themselves for a while.

"The Pope is attempting the impossible," was their emphatic opinion.

And in a rush of certainty they said: "We dare not lay ourselves open in this way. Till now no Protestant has ever been canonized. In fact the Church has never yet canonized any mortal because of his works of art."

"That would be no objection," said the Bishop of Hamburg, "because we know that the Roman Church esteems achievement; and Gregory has stressed the concept of achievement in such a way as though, in the case of Bach, its application should be extended to works of art."

"In the struggle over the unification of the two churches," someone said, "for that in the last resort must be Gregory's ultimate object—we dare not yield an inch of ground."

"But who is yielding ground?" cried the Bishop of Oldenburg. "It seems to me that at the moment it is the Pope. For the tradition of the Church of Rome is more stubborn than our own; and the opposition of the Cardinals will be stronger than our opposition, to which I also subscribe."

"Then you too are convinced that this is just a purely personal idea of Gregory's?" asked the Bishop of Hamburg.

"I am," the Bishop of Oldenburg replied.

"Then we must try to pronounce on this in the same manner as his Cardinals."

And later, when they were again seated before the Pope, what the Bishop of Hamburg said was this: "Who would not be fired by Pope Gregory's stirring idea? Even his first letter made it obvious to me that our two minds were indeed close. In the center of our conception of the active, worshiping person was the creativeness of the artist. We all of us realize that in Johann Sebastian Bach art has attained its ultimate, unique, supreme order. His Holiness Pope Gregory has made the point better than I can, when he said simply that the principle of paying homage to God, of adoration, is inherent in Bach's music. That, we venture to assert, once and for all establishes the nature of Bach's art. He was an artist and he was a devout Protestant. Your Holiness must realize that; though of course, Your Holiness knows that it is so. We, however, will only concern ourselves with the artist, so as not to extend the problem. The monk, the saint, the artist, are different concepts, different ways of life. Bach was no monk; for in the course of his earthly life he had two wives and by them a host of children. He changed his place of abode frequently, solicited posts and distinctions. He practiced his art. Neither was he a saint. For the saint lives, as does the monk, his whole life through in the stern consciousness of God, and this he receives clearly only because he avoids, or repents, each work that aims at worldly success. That, however, was the aim of Bach's art. What also troubles us is the fact that the Roman Church places the saints in heaven; despite our great human ignorance it indicates to its faithful followers those whom it says are saints; the Lutheran, however, stands before the forum of the Christian heaven with prayer alone, and to him that heaven is not graced by saints, nor even by the Virgin Mother of the Lord.

Thus we converse only with Christ, with God; before Him
alone we make our decisions and to Him alone justify our
conduct. Bach himself stood before this forum as a person and
as an artist. Man is judged not by man, but by God alone.
We are left the artist, and that should suffice. His art is avail-
able to all. No earthly experience can move us more than
the performance of his works. His art has the power, of which
he himself sang, that it 'destroys the works of the devil.' His
star will never set. And though impermanence is inherent in it,
as in all things earthly, yet it will be easy for God on the Day
of Judgment to take the music of Johann Sebastian Bach into
the new and better world which he will establish, as being the
most wonderful fruit of man's creation. That we know, and it
needs no special gesture on the part of Rome to confirm it . . ."

The Bishop stopped. Gregory was gazing at him steadily,
his eyes slightly startled. He had been sure that in his answer
the Bishop of Hamburg would go part of the way to meet him.
His hopes seemed completely dashed, for this was the final
word against his plan and the only objection, if political and
confessional considerations were being disregarded, at least out-
wardly. By itself, it was a theological objection, and it weighed
more heavily than all others. It was a short while before Gregory
could answer the Bishop. In the end he collected himself and
said: "When I have made my ideas known to the Holy Office in
Rome and I have been granted the right to propose Jean-
Sébastien Bach for canonization, then a tribunal will be chosen
which will try my candidate's case. And in all probability I
shall not be able to carry it through. Yet I tell myself now, as
before when I was at school and rational doubts of my belief
sprang up within me: *Credo quia absurdum.* And then Our
candidate will be allotted two advocates, a devil's advocate
and a God's advocate. And the devil's advocate will raise

exactly the same objections as have just been advanced by the Lutheran Bishop of Hamburg."

Pope Gregory stopped. There followed a silence which they all felt embarrassing. Then Gregory went on: "We asked you to come to Rome so that We might impart to you Our innermost thoughts and sentiments, and We would wish you to participate once We have won the struggle with Our own theologians. We have no mental reservations and nothing else in mind than to put into effect the idea which I here imparted to you. We do not feel strong enough, nor that We are called upon to carry through the longed-for reunification of the Church divided. But We will do what lies in Our power. And so We will ask it of God, and will thank Him for giving Us the opportunity to advance the matter one small step. For we shall be affording Him a pleasure if one day both Confessions jointly hold the festival that We would like to set up in honor of Bach who always glorified God alone, even though he, as has been asserted, sought worldly success. So, too, did the Apostles who journeyed the world to confirm the congregations of the faithful in all countries—and St. Paul would have used Our limousine if it had been at his disposal, merely in order to hasten on the work. The history of the Church ought to have taught you that it has canonized people of quite different kinds, people who were to a far greater extent out for worldly glory than was the artist Johann Sebastian Bach. We shall withhold their names, wait to name them, until We are face to face with the *advocatus diaboli*."

Gregory stopped. A perceptible movement ran through his audience. People shifted in their chairs; some turned their heads and whispered together. The Bishop of Oldenburg spoke with the Bishop of Hamburg. They exchanged a few concise sentences.

"Well," said the Pope, "have you anything to say?"

The Bishop of Oldenburg rose to his feet, pointed across the heads of his colleagues to the waiting Pope, and said:

"There is none we would rather assist in this work of peace, this work of unification of our Churches than Pope Gregory. To whom would we entrust it, whom would we wish to do it, with whom would we once more sit down together . . . ?"

Gregory waved his hand deprecatingly.

"We intend to stay humble," he said. "Help Us in Our little work, for no one is less able to take on a greater work than We. Art is the most beautiful of man's visible works. When issuing from blessed hands, it can be a power for good like the power of the Holy Scriptures, like the phenomenon of saintly people. Yet this world pursues an evil course. Even the arts, long the most faithful sisters of the Church, now bear a discordant, divided face. Something is needed to save them. Would this not be it?

"An artist can well be a saint. Saint is not the opposite of any sort of person, unless of the wicked, of those possessed by demons. For the saint is he who has lived agreeably to God. Saintliness is not a profession, nor is it a question of being chosen. Every artist, be his art pure or demoniacal, can decide for or against a saintly life. Therefore it would certainly be wrong to pronounce an artist a saint merely because he excelled as a man. No one wishes that. We are well aware how close to profanation the idea will seem to Our Catholic brethren, when We propose Jean-Sébastien Bach for canonization. And yet We shall say the same to them as We have said here. Give me your agreement and make this act, so necessary before the history of the world and that of Grace, that much easier for me."

They postponed their decision. They broke up in silence.

There still remained the evening with the last concert, and
Pope Gregory was not admitting defeat. One or two of the
Germans even gave him a kindly smile of assent as he walked
quickly away, holding himself very straight.

Hammerschmied watched him thoughtfully until he disappeared round one side of an open door with a movement
that was young and active.

A man in religious habit, yet with the face of a layman,
came up to Hammerschmied. It was one of the brethren who
provided the service in the house. He brought a letter which
the Bishop, whom it reached at lunch time on the terrace
looking over the park, opened with agitated hands. It was from
Luise. She was waiting at an inn in the street, and asked if he
would go to her. Hammerschmied went, a happy smile on his
face, effacing all trace of worry. In the green bower of a res-
taurant garden enclosed by trellises he found Luise, in a sum-
mery dress, with some music and a raffia bag under her arm;
she was looking ascetic, her face thinned by the sun of the
Roman summer.

"You here—and at this time?" Hammerschmied said.

"Are you in a hurry?" Luise asked, looking up, expectant and
anxious.

She had come from Rome with a bus that had brought
sight-seers and pilgrims. Sounds of foreign speech were to be
heard. In between his fully occupied hours the Pope still had
to contrive the audience which he was according to the new
arrivals.

"What's happening, what does the Pope want of you?"
Luise asked. "Has it been magnificent? Are you pleased? Has
it come up to expectations? Will you be sad to leave?"

"Grave questions have been put to us, Luise."

The slope dropped away steeply beneath them to Lake Alban. Clouds strode across the ridge of the hills, dispensing shadows and cooling the wind which came off the sea to find its way into the valleys. Yet neither heeded the loveliness of it. Luise took her father by the arm, raised her face close to his, and looked at him, lips opened inquiringly.

"Can't you tell me?"

"I want to."

That she was there now made him happy. His own flesh and blood. His daughter. Token of his earth-boundness and also token of his submission to God's will. Now, did these Roman Catholics have a continuing destiny of their own? Could their own blood ever give them that, as it did the Protestants through parenthood? Did the origins of their Church? The cornerstone that was their devotion to God's will? Here, however, it was a matter of the whole grave business of being man, the application of a whole existence to God.

So the words rolled from his heart like heavy slabs of stone. It was not that he had any urge to talk about it. He had done that for hours and hours with his colleagues. And they had decided. They were not going to stop saying no to the Pope; having got into the trap they would be stubborn; all their measures were defensive ones.

Had Luise really come to ask about this? Had she an inkling? Was this the idea at which she had hinted in Rome a week before, when she said that she knew what the Pope wanted of them? Hammerschmied told her without hesitation. He said: "Pope Gregory wants to canonize Bach."

"My God," exclaimed Luise softly and put her hand on his.

"We know no more," he admitted.

Her eyes were sparkling with enthusiasm.

"You don't know more? But do you need to know more with

Pope Gregory? Do it, for heaven's sake; do it, say yes, don't fail at this moment. Don't fail in this unique hour."

"Do you know what you are saying?" Hammerschmied asked calmly.

"Yes. Gregory is an important man. Make use of this opportunity. Another will never present itself. Saint Johann Sebastian. And if you won't, or can't, do it for the sake of our faith, of the Lutheran Confession, then do it for the sake of the unbelieving, of the masses who cannot or will not believe, who trample everything underfoot. Pope Gregory is making it possible, making it possible for once to do what so many have always wanted, whether they knew it or not: to force everyone, even the most ignorant peasants of Germany, Spain, or Italy, to their knees before Johann Sebastian Bach, before Art. Father, do you know what that means?"

"And you have nothing else in mind?"

"Oh, many other things. But let this one consideration suffice. Don't put obstacles in his way, help him! If anyone has deserved to have friends, it is he. Here on earth. For in heaven he has certainly one Friend."

"So you too believe that?"

"And you?"

"I," said Hammerschmied, "I suppose I must believe it too."

"Then help him!" Luise urged eagerly. "I will come back to Germany with you to win support for this man's idea, as well as I am able . . ."

Three hours later they were all seated for the last time in the chapel of the papal residence: the young—for his office far too young—Venetian Cardinal, and the two Benedictine monks; the six Lutheran Bishops from Germany; two renowned musical experts, lecturers at a university in southern Germany

—Christians of the Evangelical Confession, whom Pope Gregory had invited to come and share with them those last hours of devout musical fulfilment. He appeared, violin in hand, a virtuoso in white raiment, with the hair of an old man, the papal cap on his head and on his finger the Fisherman's ring: GREGORIUS XIX. PONTIFEX ET ARTIFEX. He played the E major Suite for violin by Johann Sebastian Bach. And he had decided that when he had finished playing, he would address no further appeal to his guests. Whether he had convinced them or not, he was prepared to go his way even without them. The first step, that of presenting the idea before the Roman Catholic forum, had already been taken; the Venetian Cardinal was still there and also the two monks, and Gregory had told them the idea in a few words shortly before the hour of the concert. They had agreed unreservedly, been humbly enthusiastic. As he now appeared before his audience, he was feeling more confident than he had that morning.

Gregory put the violin to his chin, raised his bow, let it sink slowly, drew a couple of strokes—and then glorious music poured out. Masterly and assured, he played the piece to the end. The look they saw on his face seemed one of transfiguration.

The music was finished. Gregory lowered his head and left the chapel, walking quickly. The men rose to their feet in silence, one after the other, and followed him. He was standing outside on the paving stones, surrounded by the monks and the Cardinals who were wearing their ceremonial dress. Black and scarlet went well together. A castle of noble walls, colorful battlements, impressive flags stood in established, seemingly invincible splendor. The Germans kept at a suitable distance. Then Bishop Hammerschmied stepped forward and walked hesitantly up to the Pope and stopped in front of him. He seized his hand, drew it up to his lips, and kissed the Fisherman's ring. His friends stood irresolute. They seemed to be viewing the scene through eyes that were dimmed, yet all at once it seemed to them real and right and good.

"We thank you," said the Bishop of Hamburg, his breath catching. "Indeed, we thank you . . ."

It was touching to hear how he sought for words, for simple words in order to avoid the heavy, worn-out ones, and in this he succeeded and at the same time failed.

"We shall go back to the north and tell of you, speak for you. May God the Almighty guide your plans in accordance with His will!"

CHAPTER 11

Pope gregory's car left the mountains. The engines of cavalcade resounded in the valleys. Country people, at work in the fields and on the slopes, looked up, stepped in astonishment out of the shadows of rocks and trees, and stood in the dazzling morning sun of high summer to look after the gleam of metal and paint and the cloud of dust. They were busy on the steep slopes on which the low ranks of olive trees were arrayed, cutting grass with their sickles in the dry valleys, and at work in the fertile vineyards lower down. Gregory was driving to Rome, to his Cardinals, to attend a session of the tribunal judging the two candidates who had been put forward for canonization. It was St. Augustine's day; and also Gregory's birthday. His people awaited impatiently. They had promised themselves that the Pope would be especially gracious, hoped that with his help they would that day be able to confirm both candidates.

Gregory, however, was intending to surprise them in quite a different way. He had been in a happy mood as he got into his car in the courtyard of his summer residence. As soon as Ernest, his chauffeur, had driven off after the roaring motorcycles, the Pope had wound down the side window so that a draught of fresh air struck his face as they drove along, round hairpin bends and curves, over gullies and dry watercourses, beside groves of olives and treeless precipices. Air kept pouring into the car, in waves, in floods, in thin trickles that had no great effect, yet ever and again changing, coming now cool, now warm, sometimes hot. Whenever the car had climbed a height from which you looked down over the broad lands of the Campagna, the wind was cool and refreshing, but in the gorges and valleys, where Gregory could not see the ridge of the hills and his eyes could no longer discern the foot of the gorge, the air was heavy and hot; the car clove through it, sucking it inside through the open window.

The Pope shrank from its fierceness; he felt perspiration on his forehead, held back his breath, which was hot and rose to his head, felt his blood becoming more sluggish, until it seemed dammed in its course and about to cease to flow. Avid for coolness he opened the other window as well.

As soon as they were out of the gorge, he sat back quietly. Now a fresh breeze again blew into the car; he laid his hand on the top of the glass, looked out at the countryside and mused. A new wave of heat came and with it fierce light that filled the car; the sun sparkled on the front window. Gregory closed his eyes and waited till they had rounded the next bend and shadow again fell over his lids. He looked up, but his head was swimming, and the picture was not sharp; the landscape was sinking. He pressed his hand more tightly on the edge of the glass, suddenly let go and clasped his forehead on which perspiration had broken out strongly. He wiped it off with the back of his hand, leaned his head a little way out of the window and drank in the air, warm though it was.

Gradually it became cooler, and a bend in the road brought the car out over the expanse of the countryside; the wind audibly rustled the stiff leaves of the olives along the side of the road. But Gregory already felt so weak that the motion of the car troubled him. He closed his eyes. But again the perspiration broke out, not because of the warm air this time, but forced out onto his brow from within, where his strength had failed him. Breathing became difficult. As he unclenched his hand from the edge of the window he felt a pricking as of a hundred needles. His hand seemed to have become heavier, the nerves in it grown numb; he could no longer bend his fingers. He tried to bend those on his other hand; they refused to move. Then he raised his arm, lowered his head, and wiped the beads of moisture off his forehead with the silk of his sleeve. He called out softly for Ernest to stop. The car slowed down, left the road, and came to a standstill. The motorcyclists also halted and their drivers shut off their engines. Ernest and two men hurried to him.

Weakly Gregory waved them away, and as soon as Ernest had opened the door he raised himself with one energetic heave out of the car, staggered, and found support on the shoulder of one of the men. The weakness made him tremble once more, then his strength slowly returned. He was again able to open his eyes, gradually the joints in his hand could be moved. He freed himself from the men and took a couple of steps alone. Little by little walking became easier; even his thoughts were more lively. He went further, left the road, and stepped across the ditch beside it at the foot of the slope. The road had left the hills; there were only one or two low spurs, covered with grass and olives, and up one of these mounts of olives he started climbing. He walked along with

ease, began to appreciate the heat of the sun again, and from
the top of the hillock, which was bare to the northeast, he had a
good view.

There lay Rome; the whole country ran toward it like a
disk sloping inward, on the rim of which, like the blunted
edge of the world, lay the extinct craters of the hills. Gray,
dried-up greenery predominated, and the Pope's white garment
brushed plants and grass, sand and stone, the hard, gnarled
cartilaginous branches and trunks of the olives. Already his
companions were out of sight, both men and machines. His
ear could no longer distinguish the voices of his outriders from
the calls and scraps of conversation of the peasants. He was
away from the road, away from his office. Never had Rome,
where his Cardinals awaited him, been farther off than at that
moment. As remote as once in his monastery in Burgundy, as
remote as in the land of the Basques when, on the way to
school, he had run off onto the white sand of the shore, where
the roar of the sea had bewitched the boy who was already in-
toxicated with music.

In the background had been the reddish-brown mountains
of the Pyrenees, shutting off the whole visible world lying
beyond. The eye could discern no way through, no valley
mouth, not even the cranny of a ravine through which a
needle would have passed. Yet the open sea was near. The boy
found a shell and took it in his hand. With it, like the lad
whom St. Augustine once found on the shore, he wanted to
empty the sea. The waves came rolling up, more and more
waves coming up together and covering the shore far and wide.
The boy could not get the better of them; they spattered his
body and shrouded his sight. Each time he fled helpless up
the beach. Calmer water followed, yet always strong enough
to cover his legs up to the knees; and when he hastily ran

back with his booty, the surf caught him up and he spilled his catch. His endeavors threatened to grow tedious, so he stopped and stood there testing and watching the hissing foam. He measured with his eye how far up the beach the tongues of surf licked, then dug holes in the granular sand all along the shore. The next time the surf came and the foam had run up and flowed back again, it left pools in the holes. The boy linked them all, one with another, and made canals into the hinterland, and into them the sea ran. Yet when he then moved from one pool to the other, the sun and the sand had drunk all the water up. Then he went back to his shell, hid it, and continued on his way to school.

Even as a boy he had always found the strength of mind to correct himself, not to let himself go wandering off, however much he would have liked to have gone. Now, valuing the little strength that he possessed and being too sensible to squander it, he asked himself whether it was right to want to empty the sea. St. Augustine had known that it was impossible when he found the boy busy trying to do it. And Augustine was a wise, saintly man, whom you could trust, and he had saved the ignorant boy the trouble. For that is what saints are for.

Having developed that thought to its end, Gregory told himself that in a couple of hours he would be facing his Cardinals.

"As soon as I have divulged my plans to them, I shall have to vindicate myself. Have I really avoided becoming obsessed with this idea? Have I strayed off the one, possible path? Are not other tasks perhaps more urgent than the canonization of Johann Sebastian Bach? Dare I hold the Church back while I busy myself trying to empty the sea? The Church's plan is fixed. There are things which appear more necessary than devoting time to mere play. The two processes which the consistory is now conducting for the canonization of my predecessor before last and that martyred German nun are both of sober logical consequence. Here are two people who, as children of God, in unwearied toil and constant prayer, devoted their lives to God and to the Church which is God's body, not God's house. Johann Sebastian, however, filled the house of the Lord with praise, with one great lovely *Laudate Dominum*. Not more? Is it not enough? But I cannot say to my Cardinals that music is also equivalent to the body of God; and because I cannot say that, I shall not be able to accomplish anything. The time is not yet ripe. My ideas are but grains of seed which the wind scatters, mere waves in the sea which no boyish hand can bind."

While thinking this, Gregory walked down from the hillock and came out below the tortuous road by a little stone bridge, at the sides of which the flooding stream had spread smooth swirls of sand. Tracks of birds and children, crows' feet and ball of foot, heel, toes, were delicately impressed there. They ran straight across, hesitated on the bank, where they scattered, then leaped across and continued on the other side, up the slope to the road.

There was that nun whose life Power had violently ended. Quietly she had spent her days in the convent during her latter years, after the robust course her life had taken before she took the veil. Countless friends had been hers; she had rivaled men in the arts and sciences. She had lectured on the philosophies of the previous century, since once the State had called her to the university and charged her with that. Later, however, she recognized that even the State could not make it possible for people to live their lives in the four main virtues; rather did it obstruct the powers which man is given to help him strive toward God.

So she had given up the post, in which the State had put her, and at the same time left the circle of the arts, of science,

and gone to the source of the one learning: the teaching and
doctrine of our Lord. All whom she had forsaken, pupils and
friends, followed her and knocked at the convent gate. They
gained admission and a hearing. The sister had to keep her face
concealed behind bars and was watched by two old nuns, whose
knitting needles clicked tirelessly, while the visitors waited and
listened. She sent no one away. When asked, she told the
truth to the best of her knowledge. Then came the overthrow
of the State. Suspicion reigned. The new autocrats, inhuman
and dark, comparable to the evil powers of Oriental legend,
held it against the forces of God that they had given their
services to the old State, which now was overthrown. They
feared that the forces of God were still exerting an influence:
in private houses where they gathered disciples round them,
those who had been removed from public colleges; in theaters,
where they took the roles of actors; in the darkest recesses of
monasteries where, hidden from the world, the mysterious
science, the magic of truth, still spun its threads. And so they
took them away: professors and writers, monks and nuns. Not
all, just a selected few, those whom they felt to have seen
through them and put them to shame. They hanged them and
burned them. And this in the middle of the twentieth century
after the birth of Christ, the century that had also given birth
to Pope Gregory. Among the victims—men and women, Jews,
Christians, and unbelievers—was the nun on account of whom
Gregory was that day driving toward Rome and his Cardinals.
She was a saint. For she had been granted the fate of God on
earth.

That was to be sealed in Rome that day. The canonization
was to take place at Christmastide. The way of the Church
was a straight and a proud way, that led on toward the triumph
of Christ returned. Already the mighty pillars of His throne

were standing. And it was to these great figures at the altar of
the Church that Gregory wished to add his musician. Him too
they should number among the saints, that he be honored
equally with the others: Johann Sebastian.

What would they say?

Gregory turned his steps upward toward the road. He had
gone quite a distance from where he had left it. His companions
were waiting higher up, by the bend.

Now he felt that he had not the courage. It was, perhaps,
only the weakness which had overcome him in the car, but now
he had doubts. He questioned his ideas, all he had so far done.
He already felt that he would be unable to summon up the
strength to express his ideas to the Cardinals. It would be the
same as, when a boy, he came late to school and told his teacher
that he had had something better to do than to come to school:
he had spent the time on the beach emptying the sea with a
shell. He had even built a great system of canals and it had
taken a lot of work to complete it. Mocked and laughed at,
the grownups had accounted him a fool!

Gregory reached the car. The men stood waiting and looked
at him questioningly. They did not know which it would be:
on to Rome or back into the hills. Gregory seated himself
in the car and with a finger gestured in the direction of Rome.
At that they hurried to their places, mounted, and set the
motors thundering.

The two advance riders closed up with the car, Ernest regained his driving seat; and so Gregory drove to Rome, leaning
back on the cushions, with his energies collected once more and
determined to suppress any fresh weakness, even that of his
own thoughts. Half an hour later he entered the streets of the
Eternal City and was cheered by the awaiting people.

They knew that the Pope was coming to Rome. It was St.

Augustine's day, the day on which the Pope celebrated his own birthday. He was coming to Rome to receive the homage of his Cardinals and at the same time to consult with them. A large number of dignitaries had gone to the Vatican early that morning. One car after the other had driven up, the last being that of the Pope escorted by the four black-clad motorcyclists, past the steps of St. Peter's and into the courtyard of the Vatican. Groups of spectators had gathered before the entrance, on the steps of the cathedral. They watched the cars arrive, bringing Cardinals, bishops, abbots, and patriarchs to greet the Holy Father on his birthday. When one car had passed, they waited patiently for the next, which came perhaps ten minutes later. One or two were even able to name the people as they drove past in threes and fours in their cars. Many of the dignitaries sat alone, leaning back comfortably behind their chauffeurs. There were white beards and smooth faces, the bare cropped head of a Benedictine abbot, the abbot of a Cistercian monastery dressed, like the Pope, in white, the patriarch of the eastern Church, purple bishops, scarlet Cardinals, Europeans, Americans, Asiatics. All the important men of the Church who happened to be in Rome came to the Vatican. And then, too, faces from the civic world of Rome: the President, mayors, people of the nobility, who of old had access to the Vatican: relatives of the Cardinals, diplomats with members of their families. And they all drove away again after the ceremony, while the others went into the tribunal, to wait patiently for what Gregory had to say.

CHAPTER 12

A N EVENTFUL DAY, the birthday of the Holy Father. It was
both the theologians' present to Gregory, and his to
them. The success of the two processes, however, was a fruit
of the Holy Ghost: the last Pope but one and the nun Gertrude
were to be canonized. Having confirmed the dual canonization
which the procurator had won, Gregory said to his theologians:
"Our trouble has borne fruit. It has been a lengthy way of
glorifying the candidates to our children, calling them happy
and holy, salutary examples for any of the faithful. Yet let us
remember once more the toil these saintly people took upon
themselves during their lifetimes. We have often felt urged to
intervene in the two processes, to speak the final word and to
confirm your decisions. Our hesitation has been a stumbling
block to you; yet let us be honest and for once examine our
feelings: can we help feeling a considerable aversion to making
the lives of these persons, whom God has favored, objects of
so complicated and grandiose proceedings as of old have been
prescribed and customary in the Holy Church? The documents
of canonization proceedings lie by the hundredweight in our

libraries. One might think that the kingdom of heaven consisted of heaps of paper. And yet it should not be . . ."

Pope Gregory paused. Before him stood his advisers, who had risen to their feet as the Holy Father entered the hall. Gregory was standing slightly to the side of the lectern, and he used the pause to give them the sign to sit down with a little golden hammer. He tapped it once on the lectern: judges' consultants, plaintiffs, informants, attorneys, advocates, witnesses sat down again. Many were in the garb of higher dignitaries; many were monks. The spectators' gallery was filled with ecclesiastical birth-day guests and Vatican officials: Cardinals, some foreigners among them, who had come to Rome for that day's ceremonies. All these faces Gregory suddenly saw; it was as though a veil had fallen from his eyes as he looked at them, his gaze passing above the heads of the theologians. He saw a fleeting smile come into their expressions, sensed in many of them a cold, almost icy curiosity, and their eyes looked at him questioningly . . . His thoughts became almost confused at the realization, brought home to him by his own words, that he was now going to let these lengthy, exhausting proceedings, with their concen-tration on logic and dialectic, be followed by a similar one, far more difficult, on Johann Sebastian Bach. Worthless piles of documents would in the end form a counterweight to the tower of scores in which the heaven of Bach's music stands recorded. If, Gregory said to himself, if even these perishable sheets of music were unnecessary in heaven, where there was no need of them since all the music that they sang day and night before God's throne was written in the heads of the angels, how much less need must there be for the documents of these canonization proceedings. They were a poor substitute for God's memory: there were no processes in heaven.

This then, concluded Gregory suddenly, was how the work of the Holy Ghost appeared: a trial with records and documents as in any mundane court. Would the Day of Judgment be like that? He did not think so. Then He will have returned and be standing there. And He will be the touchstone, and all will prostrate themselves; they will turn away, because they cannot bear His brightness; or they will stand there and bear it; and these latter will be the righteous. Will be the chosen of all those judged.

Pope Gregory closed his eyes before he went on.

Still he hesitated. As he looked up, he again saw the faces of the theologians, large and close, all turned toward him, inquisitive, ironical, expectant. He looked at them one after another. Many dropped their eyes, others looked back questioningly, but with determined expressions. It appeared to be a challange, and he felt himself challenged to speak. Yet he still hesitated.

At that moment the young Venetian Cardinal stepped out from among the guests, came across to the Holy Father, and put his face close to his ear: "We await the declaration, Holy Father. The Holy Office has for several days been informed exactly of what happened in Castel Gandolfo. We therefore beg Your Holiness not to hesitate . . ."

The Cardinal stepped back. Gregory lowered his head, clasped his hands at his breast, and looked round him. Before he went on speaking, in a flash there passed once more through his head all the reasons which had induced him to have the artist Johann Sebastian Bach pronounced a saint before an ecclesiastical court. Firstly, there had been those moods in which he had invoked Johann Sebastian Bach as a saint. Slowly the idea had taken shape, had attained clarity, like an object that you can make visible. Then he had invited the Lutherans, of whom Bach had been one. And they had come. Talks and conversations had

followed. And then, just recently, hesitation. Yet fresh hope had
come, and as a final motive there were its three advantages: it
would set an example for mankind; it would show artists the
point of departure, and so set them back on a course from which
they had departed; it would help to prepare the reunion of the
divided churches. All that could only be a feeble beginning.
Everything was merely provisional, even Bach; for he could not
with his own strength invest his works with eternal life; God
must occupy Himself with them and had already done so. Thus
Gregory dared speak, dared say what he longed to say. Yes, he
must: even though he were indeed convinced that to make
Bach the object of a process in the canonizing Church could
not make Bach's star any brighter. Now they had themselves
forced him to speak: the stone had been set in motion.

What he wished to say, however, was pure and true, it was
a matter of fact, and not to be invalidated; no one would be able
to endanger, let alone destroy it, even though laughter itself
might be the result. At that moment, before he began to speak,
Pope Gregory told himself that fundamentally there was no
longer any need of a process: his word, loudly and clearly pronounced, was sufficient to make reality of what till then had
been a captive, hovering idea. Say that word, and it would find
its achievement.

And then Gregory spoke, quickly, with assurance, without
pausing, in a clear voice, with well-articulated words. The eyes
behind his strong glasses looked large and fixedly in one direction; now and again, however, they took to brisk movement
and traveled across the audience; they caught on the im-
penetrable gaze of one theologian and threw him into confusion, moved slowly back toward the exit from the hall, as
though fetching thoughts and sentiments from afar.

Pope Gregory spoke of art and of the great share it had

once had in the rise of the Christian Church. And before coming to his real theme, for which the initiated in the hall waited impatiently, he invoked the spirit of Philip Neri, the saint. He, too, had been a great artist before the world and the Lord, one who was filled with the great serenity, who had not wrestled for God in great despair but, secure in his humanity that was subordinated to the works of the Lord, had known that from youth onward God had comforted him. He invoked the spirit of Fra Angelico, and now even those not already initiated sensed that with this clearly constructed, well-substantiated speech the Holy Father was preparing a surprise that would challenge their opposition. Those already acquainted with his intention, however, looked him openly in the face. For them this speech had lost the worst of its sting; the surprise had already been taken from it. They were just waiting in suspense for the Holy Father to express the essence of his idea, as he had done to the Lutherans. To some of them, however, his intention appeared outrageous. They felt choked, and, if they could, they would have left the hall and gone back to their offices. But they told themselves that it was their duty, meet and right, to point out his errors even to such a man as the Pope. So they let the Pope speak and held their peace.

Meanwhile Gregory was feeling how great was the difference between this occasion and the previous one in Castel Gandolfo when he had spoken to the Lutherans. The calm intellectual atmosphere that had mainly prevailed there had here added to it a portion of robuster judgment. Here sat no sober, black-garbed Northerners, but his Cardinals, bishops, and prelates in their purples, pinks, and scarlets. Various were the expressions on their faces. There were the gray eyes of Cardinal Secretary of State Hopkins. He showed the Pope an open, anxious countenance; at times he turned his head and Gregory saw his handsome firm profile. There shone the fair head of an Irishman, the white hair of a Spaniard, and among the bishops there were even two Asiatics, an Indian and a Chinaman, who, expelled from their countries, had lived in Rome for decades. Then there were the prelates, some of whom were about the Pope every day as chamberlains, stewards, masters of works, and in many other capacities. Lastly there was his father confessor, the French monk who, to appease the Cardinals had also been at Castel Gandolfo and who had long since been informed of the Pope's plans. These, then, were the fronts, the division of the audience in the hall of justice, which the Pope found himself facing. He stood before them, turned now to this group, now to that. He held his hands at his chest, often lightly clenched, and you could see that they trembled. He was not smiling.

He had already been speaking for nearly a quarter of an hour and was almost at the end of the first part of his statement, which was to be followed immediately by a second with the actual avowal, when from among the spectators Cardinal Platoni raised his hand and interrupted the Pope. Gregory stopped at once and nodded questioningly. Platoni stepped forward, came to Gregory's side, and spoke in a whisper. At the same time a sighing wave of relief passed through the assembly.

"Holy Father," said Platoni, "assuredly it would be best to end here and to continue the discussion in a more restricted circle. As yet very few know of Your Holiness' idea; it is still not too late to avoid the tremendous sensation which the scarcely practicable plan of our Holy Father would cause."

Still confused, for he had been interrupted when in full career, Gregory looked up helplessly. He saw them, one after the other. His eyes sought his friends. Hopkins' expression never changed.

But his father confessor, the French Benedictine, smiled and nodded. The Venetian Cardinal did the same. He sat nearest to him, in full view on the front row of seats. Then, all at once, the tense expression on the Pope's face relaxed, and his mouth showed the hint of a smile. Turning back to Platoni, he shook his head, motioned him back to his seat, and said almost before Platoni had sat down: "It is Our own challenge that has brought Us to this fixity of purpose. Our work has already gone so far that it is as little possible to speak of Our wish being utterly impossible of fulfilment as of its being assured of success. The outcome, however, we leave to this high tribunal alone, to which We hereby commit Our candidate: the man *and* artist Johann Sebastian Bach."

Not a word. Slowly a murmuring and whispering arose. But none ventured to talk with another. Many whispered words and sounds to themselves, others shook their heads, most remained unmoved. Then Gregory took up the little golden hammer, tapped with it on the desk so that they had to stand up. The Pope slightly raised his right hand, spoke the formula, and gave them the blessing. Then he turned and went.

That same day, before he drove back to the Alban Hills, the Pope's faithful ones came to see him. But before them came Platoni; there he was, the first, standing with an uncommunicative, almost morose expression before the Pontifex, who thought he could see a hint of anger in the Cardinal's eyes.

"Well, my son?" queried Gregory.

He was smiling again, although he had no hopes of the visit. He took it even as a bad sign that the first to come should be just this man whom he had rebuffed a short while before, when he had been interrupted by him in his speech. None of his friends having come to him, the Pope had not yet received reinforcement from outside, and thus, as he faced the strongest man of the Church, he had to depend solely on himself.

"What words have We to expect?" Gregory asked.

"I have no words, Holy Father. No one, I imagine, can find words at this moment. No one is able to give expression to his consternation."

Then Gregory saw that the Cardinal was in a state of real distress from which he seemed to find it impossible to free himself. He appeared to find speaking difficult; his gaze was turned aside; and so they both stood, helpless, facing each other. Finally Gregory found a kindly word to say. He smiled, and Platoni saw his eyes, large and childish behind the strong glasses. He said, "Do not let yourself be disheartened. We have every reason to be much more despondent. Yet We do not want what is not possible, and from this moment We shall leave everything to the competent persons of the Holy Office . . ."

Platoni went. Shortly afterward appeared friendly faces. Gregory received them eagerly: the Venetian, a Dutch archbishop, his father confessor, and, last of them all, Hopkins, his Secretary of State. They wished him luck, expressed their readiness to co-operate. Already, they said, many were on the Holy Father's side. These sensed the one and only road it was possible to travel, that which would lead, after the canonization of Bach and his music, to the union of the Church divided.

"We want to set up a feast of peace and joy," said Gregory; "more We do not dare to hope. First, however, We have need of friends."

And he asked: "What does the tribunal think of it?"

Hopkins answered. "They are all officials," he said, "who will conscientiously open the proceedings, as they have been told to do. They are already engaged in electing the advocates. A short

while since I once again emphasized the wish of our Holy
Father, confirmed the official significance of his pronouncement . . ."

"And you?" Gregory asked him, as soon as they were alone,
"are you really entirely free of doubts concerning Our wish?"

Hopkins lowered his head and remained silent. After a while,
during which he bit his lower lip like a schoolboy, he said, looking to one side: "I too believe that Bach is in heaven . . ."

"But?"

"But whether it . . ." the Cardinal's voice caught, then he
went on, cautiously feeling his way, "but that it is absolutely
necessary to have all the stress of the normal complicated pro-
cedure, with the strain and conflict involved, that I dare not
say."

Gregory did not reply. Only later, when both were in the car
driving to the hills, did he say: "It was the only way."

Those first assurances, however, were enough for words of
thanksgiving for that day to rise up in Gregory. He uttered them
that evening. His mind and his soul were full of them as he let
himself be borne in his swift car, escorted by the four thundering motorcycles through the dusky lands of the Campagna.
That evening the vibration of the car, the ascent, and the movement on the hairpin bends of the mountains did not try him.
One feeling after the other passed through him; one thought
after the other filled his head; within him he was holding
converse with the mouth of omnipotence, and he sustained
it until the car reached its destination. Then he fled hastily
across the courtyard, to sink into quiet meditation in the gloomy
chapel, lit by only a few candles, and there he stayed for a
long time.

CHAPTER 13

THREE GROUPS HAD FORMED, which discussed Gregory's plan, three parties the adherents of which conferred and worked for or against the Pope, while Gregory stayed on at Castel Gandolfo to see out the summer and autumn. His friends met in Rome. Secretary of State Hopkins came out regularly to the Hills and reported to the Pope, or they talked on the telephone back and forth. It was an odd controversy, and it raged in Rome, in the monasteries on either side of the Alps, in the various musical centers of Europe, in the academies and universities. Enthusiastic supporters of the Pope's idea wrote advocating that it be put into effect. Already he had many friends, but the number of his enemies had doubled. These were hoping that when the spark threatened to become a fire, the discussion a public controversy, Gregory would abruptly end the discussion. For the time being, however, all the meetings of the individual factions were still being held in secret and the results did not leak out.

The oldest theologians mostly flocked around Cardinal Platoni. They were sworn adherents of that uncompromising tradition which had brought the Church so wonderfully through

the historic disturbances of the last hundred years. One or
two younger ones were also of their number, yet they mostly
kept silent and said little. It seemed that they wished to remain in the background for the time being. Nonetheless they
stood nearer to Platoni than to Hopkins and the Pope's confessor, to whom they paid merely skeptical attention. In general,
both sides had hopes of these young theologians and wooed
them. Platoni was indefatigable in personal canvassing, advocating his very definite opinions which were based both on
scholastic theology and on the realities of the Church's history,
which had never known what it means to yield. The Pope's
supporters made propaganda in the journals of the arts, science,
and literature, sought support above all through the person of
the Holy Father. Not that that was ever expressed in words,
but his picture was there—as the master—and that had its effect,
especially on the young. In his years of office Gregory had
nominated a number of Cardinals, many of them younger
men, and so on the Pope's side they felt sure of one day winning
these, though for the time being they still listened to Platoni.
Platoni was the eldest Roman dignitary and his Roman experience was far lengthier than that of the Holy Father or of his
Secretary of State. It is true that as time passed Platoni saw
some of his supporters desert him and acknowledge Gregory,
yet not in sufficient numbers to have weakened him, and he
seemed to be still the stronger. Platoni and Hopkins both tried
to obtain influence on the tribunal which was already at work.

The *advocatus diaboli* was on Cardinal Platoni's side. Material was obtained that should make canonization impossible.
Despite all attempts to influence it, the tribunal worked with
precision, though slowly and dispassionately without much
sympathy. The procurator, who was the Venetian Cardinal,
had not yet even put in an appearance, but he had sent men out

traveling through Germany, monks, musical experts from various European monasteries of the contemplative orders, who were to follow the tracks of Johann Sebastian Bach. They were well received in the Protestant parsonages, had access to all the libraries. A recommendation from the Bishop of Hamburg gave them friends everywhere; they were welcomed wherever people did not refuse to entertain the Pope's idea. They worked in Thuringia, in Saxony, and in north Germany. They went to Ohrdruf, to which Bach had come as a child, to Lüneburg, where he went as a fifteen-year-old schoolboy, to Hamburg, to which the young man Bach had come in pilgrimage to Jan Adam Reinken, venerable teacher of the organ, and to Lübeck, where Dietrich Buxtehude had been at Santa Maria's; to Weimar, Arnstadt, and Mühlhausen, where he had been violinist, organist, and leader of the orchestra; to Cöthen, where he had been director of music and conductor of the orchestra; and, lastly, there was Leipzig, where he had been cantor in the Thomas Kirche. In Leipzig two monks, organists of Benedictine monasteries in south Germany, were at work trying to discover a Catholic strain in Bach's work. There was ample: quiet preludes, humble fugues, voluntaries that could only sound as they were intended to sound, in churches of the Eternal Adoration. Then the great theology of the B minor Mass, the beginning of whose Credo—removed it is true from the lone voice of the priest and sung by many, of whom each, however, was a priest —was Gregorian. In that work he bent his knee along with the entire Roman congregation; in it Christ rises again in the utmost splendor and power, surrounded by exultant angels whose voices ring like flaming swords in what is the sole festival of the one Church now that death has been conquered—then, even surpassing it in song, splendor, and jubilation, comes the life together of the world to come, where Bach, with all the certitude of faith, puts the Holy Ghost to the loveliest, most sensitive of melodies . . .

It was on this inexhaustible strain that the assistants of the procurator, whom the Pope himself had chosen, were working— earnestly, quietly, and with the support of the third group, the Evangelical theologians whom Gregory had won over that summer.

The Lutherans were meeting a second time at Wiebrechts- hausen, the former monastery estate in the Harz Mountains. This time the representatives of the other Protestant churches, who before had not answered the call, also came.

It was autumn. The monastery was already bereft of its thick screen of foliage along the road leading from Northeim to Seesen. There were cars parked on the road and in the court- yard, cars from Germany, from abroad. There were Americans, South Africans, Swiss, Australians, poor and rich. The mansion could not house them all, and in the evenings many drove to the near-by town. The conference did not last long. When it was over, those who had been in Italy that summer stayed on, for they had to decide anew. It had not taken a majority long to declare that the Pope's plans could not be discussed; there was even talk of improper appropriation of Bach by the Catholics, and two admirers of Bach's art, well-known musical experts of the Evangelical Church, went so far as to say that Bach was not only a Protestant church musician, but also a Protestant theologian, sworn adherent of the theology of Martin Luther . . .

"Not until it has canonized Martin Luther can the Church of Rome canonize Johann Sebastian Bach or any other Evan- gelical Christian."

That was a hard statement, a blow to Hammerschmied and

his friends, a blow too to the Pope. It came out later, filtered through to the public. The originators themselves saw to that. They left Wiebrechtshausen, drove back to their residences, secure in the consciousness of having decided aright. The small Lutheran nucleus, however, stayed on to try and find a means of smoothing out the differences. They were already thoroughly familiar with Gregory's idea; indeed, they looked forward to its realization. Yet how difficult had they themselves found it to assimilate Gregory's argument. It had seemed almost impossible to comprehend the ultimate implication of the idea, and yet little by little they had come to adopt it. No one yet properly understood what they should do to show themselves equal to the occasion Gregory had prepared, but one and all were disposed to ally themselves with him and help him realize his plan. They were just relying on their own strength, and well-nigh the only reason for all this was the joy that they felt.

Hammerschmied and his friends stayed on in Wiebrechtshausen; they took counsel together while the wind scattered the leaves from the lime trees and beeches; they walked in the autumnal park, leaned against the wall of the little church which was still warm from the sun and where it was out of the wind; and hard as they cudgeled their brains they could find no way. A World Assembly, so the great synod had decided, should not be convened until those in Rome had secured a favorable outcome. They were convinced, however, that that would never happen; such was the opinion most of the Evangelical theologians held of the tenacity of the Catholic Church . . .

Before dispersing, the Lutherans held a farewell service, so that in prayer they might consider Gregory's plan once more. Then they sent a letter to the Pope telling him that his hopes were also theirs.

Did the venerable old man still have his smile? they wondered.

They were sure that he had, because he had succeeded in putting joy into the hearts of his friends. Already the numbers of those who supported him were growing. The younger Cardinals acknowledged him—those on whom his opponents had placed their greatest hopes.

"How could you!" Gregory had said with a smile.

Platoni saw his front weaken. In Rome itself the Pope's countenance influenced those who saw him frequently. Some-one produced that favorite slogan UNA SANCTA. There were discussions and articles on that theme. And though Platoni was no opponent of the movement for reunion, he said nonetheless: "Not in that way . . ."

How strongly this Cardinal must have sensed, must have feared a danger, how strong must have been his conviction of the monstrousness of the inadmissible preparations for the process. Already he had had to make a first concession, had had to give way—a little—when the date for the canonization of the nun Gertrude and of the last Pope but one was post-poned until the Easter festival. Gregory hoped to have won his process by then. How greatly, then, must Platoni, the only remaining opponent among the Cardinals with direct access to the Holy Father, have believed that he was right; how sure of his own opinion and its high responsibility, for him one day to have told one of his closest friends—Monsignore Mancini, the devil's advocate—that the thing on which he was pinning his last hopes, was that Gregory could not live much longer.

For the first time in his reign the Holy Father had taken a permanent doctor into his establishment.

CHAPTER 14

IN THE SOUTH autumn had stripped no leaves from the trees. It was spinning silvery threads and the evening gilded them; it was the festival of the harvest and the fruits were unending, with melons and grapes still filling the baskets. The Pope's residence lay midway in the course of the year: above Castel Gandolfo was a summer sky, yet thunderstorms were gathering and the conflagration of the sea glowed on the clouds; but now, toward evening a cooler breeze often came into the valleys, blowing down from the hills, and you realized that it was autumn. The sun was casting long shadows, earlier with every day.

The afternoon with its color was declining slowly; yet already twilight was bringing darkness into the grove of the dense oaks, filling it at the same time with milky vapors so that the gossamer threads became invisible one by one.

These brushed Gregory's face as he walked that evening through the garden with its trees and bushes, and often his hand went fleetingly, in a scarcely conscious gesture, to forehead or cheek where the little webs caused a tickling. Once he hastily removed his spectacles, to blink helplessly from the

gloom of the grove into the light still glittering outside. Yet
he still did not leave the grove and the hard protection of its
leaves. He walked without a book, withdrawn from the gaze of
his people, until the sunlight had gone from outside the trees
as well and a red glow had come into the west reaching from
the Campagna across the hills; an upward glance revealed the
spurs of its light on the fringe of a dark mass of cloud, growing
more and more somber toward the eastern edge of the hills.
From there darkness was coming, yet bright daylight still fell
in through the gorges and the ridges of the valleys. And all the
colors of things and plants glowed more strongly, were purer
and more positive than they were by day, when the brilliance
of the sun lay on them, dazzling and stifling them. Now there
was brightness, but no shadows; light evenly distributed over
the whole valley.

And then, as the sun was extinguished, out of the dark cloud
of the oncoming night came the moon, pale yet distinct, lying
aslant in its course, concave, to embrace the feet of hovering
Virgo who was trampling the Serpent on her crescent floor.
The streamers of fire went out; the laborers came down from
the vine-hills, back to their cottages and valleys, where the
warmth still lingered, while on the slopes cooler air was stirring
the leaves. The twigs of the ilex branches rustled as they
jerked this way and that. Dogs sent each other messages across
dips and rises, and even before the bell in the Pope's castle
had rung out its signal for evening prayer, the dusk was already
so deep that colors had been expunged and things had come
alive for the ear: plaint and jubilation of voices till then restrained. Water babbled more noisily; from the pastures sounded
the torrent of tumbling brooks, reaching the ear through grass
and bushes on which the dew was forming, dispensed by the
coolness of the evening. In the high trees of the castle perched

flocks of birds that had made a halt on their migration south-
ward. Twice in every year their great journey brought them that
way. They had lost the gift of song; their voices chattered,
then became an uproar, an excited recounting, calling, and
trilling, such as there may have been when the Lord had
finished preaching to the thousands camped by the lake at the
foot of the mountain, and they ate of the bread and fishes.
On his walk the Pope avoided that part of the gardens of
which the birds had taken possession and which they were
soiling from above with chalk-white droppings, but he had had
food scattered for them there. Now the migration of the birds
reminded him that he himself must return to the scene of his
activities . . . The following day was his last in the summer
residence.

The murmur of the fountains grew louder, and it became still
cooler. Gregory quickened his pace. He walked along the house
wall, by the ivy in which little creatures rustled, came to a
path that was paved with flags to meet his people who recognized him from his quick short steps, though in the last of the
faint twilight they could not see him till he appeared in his
snow-white raiment under the lamplights. Sisters Clara and
Raphaela, like delighted children, scuttled off down the corridor
to the Pope's room to prepare the table.

Gregory paused on the steps and looked back into the night
which had now settled on the valleys with their trees and bushes.
Slowly another world came into being, this time for the eye;
the tops of the trees altered their shape; the hills moved closer
in black profile; the moon shone as though with its own power,
although it was not nearly as bright as the radiant star that
hung above the crest of the hills. It had meanwhile assumed
dominion over all the stars in the heavens between the crest
of the hills and the edge of the cloud.

Again the bell rang. It went on ringing beyond the number of the hour and thus became a signal for evening prayer. Gregory turned and entered the little house chapel. Quiet enfolded him, a new atmosphere called into glimmering life by the candles one of the Sisters lit with long taper and holder.

Gregory stepped to the altar, in front of which a prie-dieu had been placed, bent a knee, straightened up again, and recited in a low singing voice the introduction to the suite: *Converte nos, Deus, salutaris noster.*

It was the Holy Father's last evening in Castel Gandolfo. His prayers were concerned with his own heart. The change that awaited him in the morning was unimportant; but the Pope was old and did not know whether he would be granted another summer.

The freshness of evening still burned on his forehead. It was by no means easy to dispel the pictures that had so stirred the old man's blood. After that prayer he stopped, hesitated a short while and began again:

De profundis clamavi ad te, Domine: Domine, exaudi vocem meam . . .

It was a private prayer. The Holy Father, who spoke the prayers for all mankind, was praying for himself, as had King David and King Solomon, as once the Lord did on the Mount of Olives. Yet he was not praying because he was in any distress, but rather because he realized that that was the moment in which to pray. It was like the hour of death. Do not say that so it is always and everywhere, and that to say the *Memento* is at all times required. How could Gregory, that pious, strange man, who was imbued with the most wonderful powers in the world, who had taken Bach as his model and wished to canonize him because Bach had the same value to him as had the saints of the Church, how could he have adopted the motto of St.

Theresa, whose feast was to be celebrated on the following day: "Suffer or die."

It was a hard saying. And hard too had been the life of the nun whose beatification process had recently been concluded. Those two, Theresa and the nun Gertrude, had kept the *Memento* before their eyes day after day; but not so those of whom the Pope was thinking. Johann Sebastian Bach, in the last of whose organ chorales, which he dictated to another hand, the *Memento* also sounds—how often had he not wrung joy from the strings, flutes, and F-trumpets? And Joseph Haydn, who had gaily played his music "of the middle way," not too cheerful, not too grave, as the ancient Chinese required their classical music to be; yet before each spell of work he had said the Lord's Prayer, which is itself equivalent to perfect music: not too light and not too dark, with no *Memento*, without suffering or dying. And Anton Bruckner, who laid down his pen four days before his death in order to pray; to do that he interrupted work on his last opus, in which the apotheosis of gratitude is exultantly trumpeted forth to God.

And so, too, had *his* life been: not too serene, not too harsh. He too had once ventured off the road, had hurried to the sea in order to empty it with a shell. Yet he had great discernment. He believed that he stood in converse with God, and could instance the hours when that had been especially strong. Only on few occasions had he recited the *Memento*, for he knew neither fear of death nor eagerness for it. At the same time he was humble and modest. He knew that he could err, that his own moderation was not a quality to distinguish him as Saint Theresa of Avila had been distinguished by the motto by which she had ordered her life, like an endless penitential psalm.

But on that evening Gregory too recited his penitential psalm. He besought God for understanding, to be lifted out of his contrition, for discernment of the error with which many at that time charged him . . .

Speravit anima mea in Domino . . .

A *custodia matutina usque ad noctem: speret Israel in Domino.*

But hope is joy. In hope is more joy than suffering. And Gregory's evening of reflection was followed by a morning with a bright friendly sun, whose rays made their way, warm and peaceful, through the chapel window and strewed roses on the altar . . .

Gregory came before the altar for Holy Mass. He stood before the decorated stone, on his right the side of the epistle, on his left the side of the gospel, and in the middle the tabernacle. Gregory stood with bowed head and said: "*Introibo ad altare Dei.*"

Even the altar of the Lord could have been death, to appear before which Gregory was prepared. But that made death a Mass, and passing over to God an act of communion; and in that communion would be all who were now included in his prayer: "*Ad Deum, qui laetificat iuventutem meam.*"

"*Judica me, Deus, et discerne causam meam de gente non sancta,*" Gregory went on. "Obtain justice for me, God, and conduct my cause against an unholy people."

The introductory prayers of the Mass were almost finished; the murmuring increased, became soft again. Now the Pope spoke, now his servers. At intervals thoughts flared up, like the candles on the altar, their flames straight and occasionally stooping. Gregory stood on the epistle side, whence the Church's letters to the faithful are read out, and opened the book resting on its velvet cushion. He pronounced the Introit. Recited the

Kyrie. Faltered. Felt within himself an opening that differed from the scant form of the Gregorian chant; it rose and swelled, freed his voice from its soft restraints and carried it along with it, upward and down again into the dark depths, where it touched the motto of that day's saint: Suffer or die . . . but was once more uplifted with it toward the brighter *Christe eleison:* it was Bach's melody from the B minor Mass. But it was a Low Mass which Gregory had come to say at the altar that morning. And he had actually fallen into song. He broke off abruptly, remembered, was embarrassed in front of the assistant priests, while they were startled; then he turned Bach's melody into the more familiar solemn Gregorian air, and that enabled the servers to collect their wits and respond in the corresponding choral melody. And there it stayed: Gregory had turned the Low Mass into a sung one. It was a simple matter for the servers to go to the side and, bending one toward the other, to light the charcoal for the incense and let the fragrance rise to the altar of the Lord. After the lesson, Gregory turned, having heard the reassuring clink of chain and censer, and blessed the incense. As he did so, he lightly inhaled the solemn smell and that made him think of the words in which Thomas Aquinas had prayed to the hidden God:

"Visus, tactus, gustus in te fallitur. . . ."

"Visus, tactus, gustus in te fallitur . . ." Sight, touch, taste are fallible as indications of Thee . . .

But in the smell of incense—which was even scattered before the cradle of our Lord—the mind does not deceive itself over God. The smell, too, was stimulating. In it was the smell of pastures, the smell of woods, the smell of the garden, the smell of water, the smell of creation which was like a rose and opened its petals to make the miracle manifest. There was the face that perceived the cycle of creation; there was the hand that grasped the wood of the cross and held the hand of a friend, which felt that life was in all things.

And yet, Gregory told himself, the spiritual organ, the spiritual sense, was the ear. For to continue with St. Thomas: *"Sed auditu tuto creditur."*

He wanted to have the theologians recite that hymn, when he had to present himself in Rome before their tribunal which was judging Johann Sebastian Bach. They were waiting for him with proofs of sight, touch, and taste. Yet Gregory was of good courage.

> Eye, hand and mouth failed to find Thee,
> My ear alone revealed Thee to me ...

CHAPTER 15

THE TRIBUNAL HAD ASSEMBLED. The theologians were waiting for the Pope. Cardinals Hopkins and Platoni were seated amongst the guests of the Sacred Congregation of Rites. It was known that latterly they had had several secret meetings. Now they were neighbors and, like the others, waited in silence. The proceedings had not yet progressed far. Apparently they had reached an impasse. However much the devil's advocate had sought evidence, there was nothing that spoke against Johann Sebastian Bach. The sources from which an accurate picture of his life and conduct could have been obtained had been very unproductive. His life had been so rich in works and wisdom, and latterly in saintly composure and humility as the procurator demonstrated, that the fact of young Bach having had a nasty brawl with some bassoon player or other over his betrothed, Barbara, did not weigh in the scales. No quarrel that he had had with the authorities, none of his solicitations of posts and honors, of which there was proof enough, could weigh as heavily as his work and his faith that had removed mountains. Every argument of the devil's advocate, the painstaking, precise Monsignore Mancini, who made his speech in an acrid voice, was quashed by the opposing side, in the person of the Venetian Cardinal. They were all dismissed by the judges' consultants with shrugs of their shoulders. He would have to prove things of greater weight.

The fact that in his lifetime Bach had had two wives, that he had not remained a widower after the death of the first, was inevitably an argument for Mancini, the virtues of marriage having been laid down by St. Paul, whose instruction was that widowers and widows should remain in that state. That was supposed to be agreeable to the Lord. But, after violent discussion, even this argument was defeated, for it was the argument of the Sadducees, the one with which they had tempted Christ over the Resurrection. The controversy lasted for some time, for minds had first to recover; faithfulness to the dead lies deep in the human character, deeper perhaps than faithfulness to the living. But death, so said the opposing advocate, was the province of God and no one dare force his way so far.

"But, after all, it is the dead we canonize," cried the devil's advocate.

"Because they have given us a sign that they are in heaven."

This latter argument gave rise to the situation in which the Holy Father was asked to intervene on behalf of his candidate. He had returned to Rome at the end of October, and in the second week of November he had celebrated the feast of the arch-basilica of the Saviour in his church on the Lateran. Ever since the fourth century, this church, built by Constantine the Great and consecrated by St. Sylvester in November 329, has been the mother church of all God's houses in the world. Today it bears the name of John the Baptist.

This service of the Pope's was the first since his return in which the faithful could participate. The basilica was crowded, even though it was a weekday. Many had come to hear the

Holy Father preach: scholars, students, many artists, men and women, old and young; and they all found their hopes fulfilled. Gregory addressed himself to them. It was a sermon that caused a sensation.

He spoke of the churches of Rome which had been erected on the foundations of ancient temples. He began with that church the anniversary of whose consecration they were that day celebrating; it had been built on the ground plan of the old Lateran palace. He spoke of the columns in Santa Maria Maggiore, of the columns in San Lorenzo fuori le mura, of Maria in Cosmedin, of Maria sopra Minerva. He spoke of the Pantheon, which now bore a Christian name, of the obelisks of Egypt, the triumphal columns of the heathen emperors that were now adorned with the sign of the cross. Once those pillars had stood in the daylight supporting the pediments of heathen temples; now they slept in the dusky twilight of the churches, stood there fettered, sending greeting to the liberated catacombs, like thieves crucified beside the Redeemer in order that thereafter they might be with Him in paradise.

And so, said Gregory, he wished to try to translate Johann Sebastian Bach into the heaven of the saints. And he wished thereby to make a beginning in what it would be for his successors one day to accomplish, the reunion of the whole Church, firmly based on a common foundation stone.

Once, in ancient Greece, there had been the singer Orpheus. He was a heathen artist, a magician, almost the equal of the gods; nevertheless the early Christians had associated him with Jesus Christ, thus making him almost a saintly figure. In fact, he had become a symbol of Christ: Christ—Orpheus. Now here —in Johann Sebastian Bach—Orpheus had risen again, whole, for the first time; and not as a symbol to be contrasted with the Lord, but in the company of the Lord, like St. Luke, St.

Gregory, St. Francis. There was no doubt that Johann Sebastian Bach and his works were with God in heaven.

To the simple souls, of whom there were not a few among his theologians, those who lumped all art together and reckoned it among the profane phenomena of humanity, and who must have been sorely tried as they listened to this sermon, to them Gregory said expressly: "The Lord created heaven and earth in six days. And He created man in His own image; created him to be a representation of Himself. God Himself was no theologian. God was creative. And if man were to model himself on His example, then he did so best when he was being creative. And God created man, and man art; so God also resided in works of art . . ."

Now, a day or two after this, the theologians were assembled in the tribunal, waiting for the Pope. A murmur came from the seats of the judges' consultants; the two advocates sat with inscrutable faces; many eyes, however, were on the two rivals, Platoni and Hopkins. Just an hour or two before, they had been seen together coming out of Hopkins' office.

Every morning Hopkins telephoned to the Pope and reported on official business. A few days previously, just before the usual time for telephoning, Platoni had suddenly appeared in Hopkins' room without having himself announced as usage between princes of the Church required. Hopkins looked anxiously at the other man. It was the day after the papal commemorative service in the Lateran. Platoni considered the sermon irresponsible.

"Those are the means," Cardinal Hopkins replied, "that any convent is entitled to use when it wants to have a pious dead sister beatified. They call upon the faithful, callers and passersby, to pray for her . . ."

Excitedly Platoni retorted: "We are not in a convent here."

The following day the two Cardinals met for a secret talk: Hopkins had surprisingly invited the older man to come to see him, and without first consulting the Holy Father. At that meeting Hopkins admitted that he was convinced that the Holy Father's reasoning was thoroughly dangerous. What Gregory was trying to do was to penetrate into a world where even the bravest would lose his reason. During the service in the Lateran, while preaching his stirring sermon that had impelled all the faithful, all the unbelieving to prayer, he had been in a state of euphoria. Thus, if at that moment, when nothing was yet decided—so Hopkins said, lowering his gray eyes that sat wide apart beneath a high, weather-beaten forehead—if an accident were to happen to the Holy Father, if death should surprise him in the midst of preparing his work, no successor, not even he, Hopkins, could continue that work.

"Then," Platoni asked, "you too would at once let the process drop?"

Hopkins hesitated before replying and kept his eyes lowered. It was not long since he had promised the Holy Father his love and help. Then he raised his eyes and looked Platoni in the face.

"The Holy Father," he said, "himself possesses the power of holiness which he wants to attribute to Johann Sebastian Bach. And if he is actually able to carry that through—then, as always in such cases, it would be the work of the Holy Ghost. Nevertheless, it seems to me that the Holy Father's mind is in danger. I fear for him, and I hope and believe that it will not fall to me to have to continue his work."

Platoni looked at him searchingly and flung his head back. With a determined gesture he held out his hand to the Cardinal Secretary of State and said: "Let us wait and see what the Holy Father has yet to say."

They went out together and walked to the courtroom. Platoni felt that Hopkins' admission was a finer, more serious support for his own purpose than he had ever heard from another. For Hopkins had not concerned himself with particular points, essential or unessential, but had expressed a general opinion that was moderate in its prudence and sagacity. Both Cardinals felt that there were limits to what those who believe can understand and achieve. Gregory might be in error in thinking that he could touch on things which really were outside human discernment. That the simple, saintly Francis of Assisi was a saint was not beyond the understanding of the believer, but that God should reside in works of art was not a thing that could be taken for granted; for often art was wretched, a thing of the devil. Art had always evaded man's attempts to define it, and many who had taken it upon themselves to try had come to grief on its real secrets, as the ancients realized. Poets and musicians had fallen into madness, or had ended by committing suicide. The most obvious examples lay in that cemetery by the Cestius pyramid, toward which the Pope had gestured during his first argument with Cardinal Platoni, zealous opponent of Protestantism. Art had the effect of obscure magic. In the Church, mother of wisdom, it had always served merely as attendant. It had been servant, not priest. All other art was of no use to theology, or was perhaps held up as a symbol of the struggle between Good and Evil.

On this line of reasoning Hopkins and Platoni seemed to have joined company. No one in the court suspected it as they saw the rivals sitting silent together.

Pope Gregory's face was pale as he walked in among his theologians. His step, however, was as brisk and vigorous as ever. As soon as the door had closed behind him, he nodded to the company and walked to his place. There he raised his right hand with the Fisherman's ring and stabbed the sign of the cross over the company with a light, precise movement: two fingers outstretched, thumb and two bent fingers forming a ring. Then he sat down and with the little golden hammer gave the tap that was the signal to begin.

Once again the course of the proceedings so far was summarized for all to hear, an ordered résumé which took matters up to the point where the present situation had arisen, because of which they had summoned the Holy Father.

The belief of the people had made itself heard: saints have to make themselves understood by means of signs. They must still work miracles after death. Now, had this happened with Bach, and how? This was what they asked Gregory.

"His work is all a miracle," he answered calmly.

His voice had wanted to cry that out, yet he spoke the words almost softly. He went on, spoke a little louder, slowly his voice found its strength, yet it sounded agitated. He spoke of the hymn by St. Thomas Aquinas in which he worshiped the hidden Deity.

"Sight, touch, and taste are fallible as indications of God. These are the senses with which one perceives miracles. Luminous signs, awakening from the dead, and healings of the sick, multiplication of loaves . . . the ear relies on words alone, on the annunciation. Dear brethren: what need have we of signs, of miracles . . ."

His opponents whispered: "He is ridiculing age-old beliefs. St. Theresa strewed roses before the child Jesus. Signs which the sight perceives have always counted." They were never at a loss for an objection. Then they said that a saint could not come into heaven unless he brought a soul with him, without having performed one work of proselytism, however small. From of old the power of the saints had won believers and worked from heaven on the minds of men. Had Johann Sebastian Bach, whom the Pope wished to canonize, and of whom all believers in the world were supposed to say that he was a saint, whose name it would be salutary for any to take as witness of the divine order—had Johann Sebastian Bach fulfilled this apostolic commission which Christ had bequeathed to all?

Was this the final objection?

Gregory glanced round him. Suddenly he smiled, for the first time that day. Stretching out one arm, so that the finger on his hand thrust the objection far from him, he said: "Certainly he has. Several—yes—countless people have gone to their homes after hearing his music, withdrawn into themselves, and there have thought of God. Their thoughts have amounted to prayer. And how many have not been moved first by him to live in the way of the Lord? A philosopher, poet, and teacher of false doctrines of the nineteenth century, whom we all know by name—he publicly attacked God and in his folly pronounced him dead, and, after a life of solitude, became mad in Turin—he it was who, after hearing Bach's *St. Matthew Passion*, once exclaimed, 'From this you can rediscover Christianity, should you once have lost it.' And thousands of Christian monks, who daily bring his music to life, in cells, in churches, these endorse the power that emanates from Jean-Sébastien Bach and which can be no earthly one . . ."

Already there was a buzz of assent in the consistory and this grew into open enthusiasm. People nodded and waved to the Holy Father, and he, looking round in wonderment that charmed and moved them, called Hopkins to him and whispered in his ear. Hopkins nodded and went out. Gregory gave the signal for a pause with his little golden hammer. Hopkins returned, carrying Gregory's violin case in its light canvas cover.

Gregory gave the signal again, took out his violin, put it to his chin, raised the bow . . .

The sun broke through the window. It was midday. Outside it had grown hot; after a few days of rain a late, unexpected summer had come to Rome which on the previous day had celebrated the feast of St. Martin—a St. Martin's summer. The heat had penetrated inside and the air was sultry. Nonetheless, Gregory grasped his instrument and began to play the partita of Johann Sebastian. Again sound and light began their dance; the clear notes became as visible as light; movement, dance became audible in the calm progress of the notes. Spellbound, they all watched that figure caught in the rhythm of the music, swaying to the natural time. The robe hung smooth. The head, slightly inclined to the instrument, nodded almost imperceptibly. Each time Gregory removed his bow his hand gave it a flick and he closed his eyes for a brief moment in order to recollect the order of the notes before he began again. The Holy Father had made himself his own spokesman for his candidate: when had such a thing happened except at the pronouncement of dogma in praise of the Virgin? At that moment, the great one, the Cantor of the Lord, great patron of countless believers, seemed a protégé in the hands of the Holy Father.

The first movement was at an end. Gregory lowered his violin, put down the bow, wiped his forehead with the cloth that lay on his shoulder to protect his robe, and gestured to some men to draw the dark brown curtains, for the sun was blazing through the window. Then he went on playing: the second movement, the third, the last, wonderfully majestic and profound . . .

Every now and then Gregory wiped his brow. When from time to time he looked down he could see his hands growing pale and faded despite their pigment. He felt a tingling and pricking that grew more violent. He was nearing the end. The heat was all about him, increased by the presence of many people; the fans were switched off while the Pope played. Yet the old man once again compelled the almost unruly notes of the master into strict order. Then the spirit of Bach issued forth, was released from his hands to kindle rapture and the desire for pure peace in the hearts of his audience.

There was a burst of exultant applause, from which only few refrained. Platoni lowered his head. Hopkins gave vent to his feelings, beaming at Gregory with shining eyes. Before, he had come to doubt him. Now, however, he saw his brow, his silvery hair, his great wise eyes behind the strong lenses of his glasses that gave his kindly face an expression of helplessness, saw the small, usually smiling mouth; he saw the hands, beautiful and wonderfully articulated, grasping the neck of the violin, and the bow that was held vertical. There was no doubt: the man was himself a saint. And it was as though, at that moment, theology had been defeated and the belief of the people had won the case on its own.

Gregory laid his violin aside and his smile grew broader. But it cost him a slight effort. Suddenly he clutched at the desk with hands from which all strength was draining, knocked the little golden hammer to the ground, and found support first in the arms of Hopkins and the Venetian Cardinal, who had rushed to catch him. They led him out, while the company remained silent, and took him step by step to his apartments.

He did not regain his strength that day. But, while the two men were helping him through the door into his room, with Sisters Clara and Raphaela drawing aside, scared and timid, Gregory said, speaking slowly, though with his voice under control, and only pausing at intervals for breath: "This has been an hour of trial for Art and for Mankind. It was to some extent a tensile test for Art. For it must be of divine origin. We believe that the Holy Ghost resides in our congregations. And it has been the governing force on this occasion too. We are witnesses of that. What We wished was to see whether or not Mankind takes seriously the gifts of God, of which Art comes next after Love . . ."

The doctor who was summoned, and a second doctor who was called in that evening, pronounced the Holy Father's condition dangerous. Before midnight the news of his illness was released to the world.

CHAPTER 16

Although his Secretary of State kept all business from him, Gregory's mind was filled with a thousand thoughts and cares. It was as though he were finishing his rule as Pope, dreaming it to its end on a bed of sickness. The first few days were very disturbed. He had feverish dreams and was tormented by self-reproach as soon as he awoke. He was worried about the success of his work at the same time as he repudiated it. He had wanted Hopkins to come every day to report, but he soon gave that up, for he realized that he had need to husband his strength. It was not so much that he wished to regain his strength and complete his work. He was humble, and knew that all was in God's hand. In His name, so he told himself, he would forgo the success of his dearest wish, that to which in the last year he had devoted all his strength. No, when he admitted the necessity of unqualified care of his body, to which sickness and worry had come, it was because he considered that to be in accordance with God's decree. He tried to cover up the dark hours with the warming blanket of prayer. But the blanket was thin and worn; the cold penetrated, it failed as protection, and again anxiety worried at him, like gout in his limbs. He told himself that his plans had been ill conceived, even wicked; now that he was shut away in the dark room of his illness, the picture he had of it seemed as dark as a useless negative.

Suddenly he called for one of the two Sisters, who sat praying in the depths of the room. Sister Raphaela came, stood by the side of the bed, dropped her eyes, and waited.

"Send for Cardinal Hopkins, please," he said in a low, though agitated voice. "Tell him I should be glad if he would come at once. It is urgent."

The nun went out. Clara remained. With her rosary twined round her hands, she sat at the foot of the bed and prayed for the Holy Father's recovery. The beads clicked in her hands like knitting needles in the hands of elderly mothers, or of nuns supervising a younger sister's conversation with a visitor. In the same way, too, was Gregory watched by the nuns on duty, even though he did not converse aloud with the spirits that visited him; rather was it an uninterrupted, secret converse that was not overheard. His head rested on the linen-covered pillow, face pale and surrounded with the glistening luster of a slight beard, beneath which his cheeks lay hollow, mouth drawn down in suffering. He kept his hands folded on the cover, and his dark eyes were fixed, as though to keep them from straying, on the bent joints of his fingers.

Cardinal Hopkins came in. He stood there, tall in the still taller doorway, holding himself in an inimitable way that to the Pope, now that he was on his back, made him seem even bigger, more superior. That afforded Gregory a childish sense of comfort, which was not impaired when Hopkins bowed humbly. At that moment Gregory felt a sudden dislike of being forced by his illness to leave the conduct of affairs to the young Cardinal. And he asked himself whether Hopkins would conduct them as well as he. Doubts of his own fortitude slowly arose in his mind, but these referred principally to his own plans. To be a wise ruler, you had to be upheld by an inner strength that had no need of diplomacy. Gregory raised his head, the sinews on his neck stood out, taut; he unfolded his hands and laid them on the head of the kneeling Cardinal. Then with his right hand he made the sign of the cross and blessed him.

When he spoke Gregory's voice was keen and penetrating.

"Have the strangers arrived?" he asked.

"The strangers?"

Hopkins had risen, and he looked at the Holy Father uncomprehendingly, even in bewilderment. Then he said: "The whole world knows that it is impossible for the Holy Father to give audience while he is ill."

"But the strangers—" Gregory spoke rapidly in a hoarse voice which he tried to make sound vigorous—"the strangers are to be brought to Us at once. We await them impatiently."

"No one has been announced," Hopkins replied. "People cannot express their sympathy for the Holy Father in his illness except by praying for him, and that they do ardently."

Gregory made a deprecating gesture and let his head sink back. He laid his arms outstretched on the blanket beside him.

"And what is happening with regard to the process?" he asked.

"At the moment, nothing, Holy Father. We are all agreed that we dare do nothing without the Holy Father."

Gregory nodded weakly. He raised his hand, half disappointed, half satisfied: the Cardinal was dismissed. He went away, made more thoughtful than ever by this conversation, and at once gave orders to the doctors that from then on nobody was to be admitted to the Pope, not even the house theologians. In the bulletin which he composed as usual that evening, however, he said that the Holy Father's condition had improved slightly; in fact he had found it possible for the first time to summon his Secretary of State and had discussed with him the affairs of the various departments. The Pope had been told of, and approved, the intention that the cause of Johann Sebastian Bach should remain in abeyance until he himself should again be able to follow its course.

Winter came, a new year began. Almost every day the newspapers reported on the Pope's illness. Now his condition had improved; now he was worse. Crises occurred; people were already reckoning with his death and busied with the succession. Then the danger receded somewhat, and at once people were again talking hopefully of recovery, while others speculated on the effects of a protracted illness; even the possibility of abdication was mooted. That would have been an event rare in the history of the Church, but there were precedents. In the Middle Ages a monk had been elected Pope in very much the same circumstances as Gregory's election nine years previously, and in the end, after years of good and wise rule, he had abdicated at the invitation of the Cardinals, who had only chosen him because they expected him to be incompetent. Gregory VII himself was forced to abdicate. Rumors were rife round the sickbed of the Holy Father and tales abounded, tales of such fancifulness as were utterly inconsistent with Vatican history and diplomacy.

Soon nothing more was heard of Gregory's plan to canonize Johann Sebastian Bach, which had caused such a sensation. The reports in the press, too, were less concerned with Gregory as a person than with the incapacitated head of the Roman Catholic Church, which to that day remained the greatest organization in the world.

The indefatigable Cardinal Hopkins was now the link between the public official that was the Pope, and the private

person which Gregory on his bed of sickness had very largely
become. He worked sixteen hours a day. His photograph was
published with increasing frequency. He could be seen striding
down the corridor with firm tread and angular movement of the
shoulders, holding himself very erect in his light-colored habit.
His gray eyes were grave and looked straight ahead; his thin
lips were tight shut and only appeared to smile, absently and
always rather wearily. His hair was cut short; it was still thick,
on the fair side, though with no gray in it; and where it pro-
truded from under his cardinal's hat it was bleached by the sun.
Although of man's estate, he seemed almost youthful, and in
his raiment of prince of the Church it was difficult to determine
his age. He was forty-eight, and so there seemed little reason to
suppose that he would be the next Pope. His rival was now, as
before, Cardinal Platoni, who was his superior not only in age,
but also in experience of diplomacy and Rome.

Latterly, as he went about his day's work, walking or standing,
Hopkins had felt that he carried with him knowledge that
must be kept secret from the world. He scarcely dared to think
of it, yet the foreboding often came to him, unwanted, and it
oppressed him. He could not help thinking that if Gregory did
not die of it, his illness would result in permanent mental dis-
order. He always went in fear of the dark words that he had now
heard several times from the old man's lips when he had been
summoned to him.

"Dear Cardinal," the Pope had greeted him on the second
occasion, "Easter is approaching. On Good Friday We hope
to canonize Jean-Sébastien Bach. On that day you can with an
easy mind assemble Christians of both confessions in St. Peter's.
If Our condition has not improved by then, We shall have to
call a consistory of Cardinals to Our bedside. Of course, there

will not be anything very grandiose about a canonization performed by a Pope from a bed of sickness."

"Holy Father," Hopkins hastened to say, "the feast that cannot now be lost to the Church, for we have already celebrated
it on the occasion when Your Holiness won the entire Congregation of Rites with his playing and his speech, can only be
celebrated in the presence of our Holy Father."

Hopkins left the Pope with a heavy heart. Yet despite all his
fears, he had to admit to himself, again and again, that there
was nothing irrational about Gregory. In fact there was a force-
fulness about his words that must convince all who heard them
of his will to recover, of his confidence in getting well again.
This man, the Cardinal told himself, when you saw him thus,
heard him and appreciated him to the full, was not going to
die without having completed his work.

Still greater, however, and abiding, was the doubt in the heart
of this young prince of the Church. He told himself that, compared with the visible works of virtue, even with the visible
works of art and historical events, the canonization of a person
was no great matter. It changed nothing, because it was merely
the confirmation of a fact, though of a fact decided in heaven.
It would only be something great, so the Cardinal confessed to
himself, if Gregory really were intending that of which his opponents were secretly and openly accusing him: wishing not only
to canonize a man but also to canonize music.

That was an idea, however, which Cardinal Hopkins thought
verged on the insane. And he therefore kept close guard on his
knowledge of all that Gregory had confided to him both before
his illness and since; for it all seemed to be linked with that idea,
to be aiming directly at it. Hopkins was no ordinary man, but
his duties now laid as much upon him as he could bear. And his

duties were many, grave and important; in fact, the running of the entire Church. He therefore had no room left in his mind for entering into Gregory's dreams. It was not so much his friendship with Pope Gregory that had developed, as the claims upon him of his own office, and those had nothing to do with favor or friendship. Since the beginning of the Pope's illness he had allowed himself no leisure.

Once, in one of the sick man's quiet moments, they spoke of the dangers that threatened the Church; for, indeed, Gregory had been elected at a time of crisis, and the tension had been relaxed only because of his person.

"Will it ever be possible for the Holy Ghost to turn away from the Church, be it only for a short, or even a long, period?" Hopkins asked.

And Gregory replied: "We have the Promise. One thing we must recognize, however, is that the Church as it is at this moment will not necessarily be the Church of tomorrow, as it is not that of the past. The Church once spent three hundred years in hiding; it could also go back into hiding. There are countless misgivings which we harbor. Once, in the Middle Ages, canonization used to be possible if a bishop went and bore witness for a person because he was popularly reputed to be a saint. It seemed a miracle to the faithful if ever a man, priest or saint, succeeded in leading some despairing person back to God, in driving out evil spirits. Today, however, our theologians do not have the childlike hearts that can accept unhesitatingly the miracles of which information is sent them from the people, but they must employ scientists to make scientific investigation of these mysterious happenings. The tears that an image of the Virgin Mary has wept are subjected to chemical analysis; the sick person who has been healed is taken before official doctors. Thereby the offices of the Lord's disciples and of the Pharisees would seem to have been united. We, however, ask ourselves: does God wish to win faithful hearts for Himself, or for mankind and its science?

"Thus, in our time, the Holy Father personally"—here Gregory raised a finger and a heartfelt note came into his voice— "proposed for canonization a man who was taken to God centuries ago: Jean-Sébastien Bach. Once no one would have dared oppose the suggestion of the Vicar of Our Lord. Today, however, the Pope, We ourselves, were dragged before the Congregation of Rites. You were all once in agreement, openly applauded, when We turned advocate for Our own patron. Now, however, We are fettered by illness, and for all of you that is a welcome opportunity to let this case, which has already been won, relapse into abeyance. Doubts soon arise in the minds of men, however much they may have exulted and been filled with joy. When, at the last assembly of the Sacred Congregation of Rites, We spoke and raised Our violin, the Holy Ghost was with Us, We are sure of that; now that the process has come to a standstill, and with Our end the end of Our plans is also threatened, people are saying the Holy Ghost did not assent, because fulfilment has not been accorded to Our wish. What, dear Hopkins, can be the meaning of that?"

Again Hopkins went away feeling distressed. What the Pope had first had to say had raised his hopes. Gregory almost seemed to have grown mindful of his responsibilities. But then he had reverted to Johann Sebastian Bach, and Hopkins realized once more what a personal matter this was.

What did he really want?

Waking from a restless sleep one afternoon the Pope once again called for one of the two Sisters.

He had now been in bed for three months, and hopes of his

recovery had dwindled. Even the regular visits of his Secretary of State had been stopped. That day, however, he called for him. The Sister went. Gregory waited impatiently. Hopkins came, was still in the doorway when Gregory again asked him that strange question, seemingly under compulsion, the words appearing to be squeezed out of him: "Have the strangers arrived?"

Hopkins was startled. He looked at the ground, then looked up again and asked quietly: "Which strangers, Holy Father?"

Gregory sat up.

"Hopkins, you know that We are expecting a delegation," he said, "and We want these people brought to Our bedside as soon as they arrive."

"I don't understand, Holy Father. Your Holiness could not possibly give audience."

Gregory said: "These people have no spokesman, Cardinal, even less so than the Protestants whom We had come to us in the summer. For they are not organized. We mean the un-believing, Cardinal. You know that We wish to canonize Jean-Sébastien Bach. We want to beatify music, art, which contributes to the welfare of the world . . ."

The Cardinal raised his hand and stepped hastily across to the two Sisters sitting with clicking rosaries at the foot of the Pope's bed. He took them by their shoulders and ushered them through the door and out of the room. Then he went back to the bed, bent over Gregory, and smiled at him with anxiously trembling mouth. He raised a warning finger and asked the invalid not to talk, as that cost him an effort.

"Dear Hopkins," the Pope went on calmly, "the unbelieving also have a claim on Jean-Sébastien Bach. Having consulted the Protestants, as they were entitled to be consulted, We intend also to consult the unbelieving, among whom most artists are erroneously numbered. For, fundamentally 'unbelieving' is an expression which the theologians have coined, and which does not suit most of those to whom it is applied. They will come. We are not afraid of our plans being balked from that quarter, yet the voice of these, the unconsulted, has great weight, and We must take them seriously."

Shortly after this conversation a small miracle occurred.

Pope Gregory had already been four months in bed, and it seemed certain that he would never leave it. Lately he had been afforded peace, and he knew the joys of long lying and waiting and so proved the truth of the Psalmist when he said: *"Exsultabunt sancti in Gloria, lectabuntur in cubilibus suis."*

One day, as Gregory lay quietly with his hands folded on the cover, Hopkins, whom he was not expecting, had himself announced and shortly afterward came into the room, a look of bewilderment on his face.

"Well, my son?" Gregory said and, reaching out to the little table beside him, took his glasses, put them on, and looked at the Cardinal with his large eyes that the lenses made look larger still.

"Holy Father," said Hopkins, faltering, "we have surprising news. I feel in duty bound to acquaint Your Holiness at once of what people have been saying for some days and what can now be read on the posters: a conference of those whom Your Holiness himself recently characterized as free-thinking people is to be held in Rome. This would seem to be the fulfilment of Your Holiness' idea, as it is in fact a gathering of unorganized, intellectual people, mostly unbelieving, or at least not bound to any confession."

"And what do they want?" Gregory asked.

"It has not been said whether their visit concerns the Holy Father. But it seems certain that their coming here is not fortuitous, but closely bound up with Your Holiness' plan. They are coming to Rome to give a musical festival on the occasion of the coming birthday of Johann Sebastian Bach, and this is to attract visitors from all over the world. Concerts to be given in various churches, and also in the Teatro Argentino, in the Basilica of Constantine, have been announced. It would thus seem to be an international occasion, and it would further appear . . ."

Here Gregory sat up, supporting himself with one hand at his back, and stretched the other out a little way toward Hopkins. "Cardinal Hopkins," he said, "please tell me honestly what you believe has brought these people to Rome."

Hopkins said nothing. To Gregory he seemed to be gazing shamefacedly at the floor. It was in fact difficult for Hopkins to decide on all matters that were properly the Pope's, especially since he had had to shoulder all business of Church and State. He loved the Pope. He had to thank him, both for his career as Cardinal and as Secretary of State, and for a number of great and happy, human and spiritual experiences. For Gregory had given richly to all who had been near him during those last nine years, to Hopkins, perhaps, most richly of all. At this stage, however, apart from a few monks and the Venetian Cardinal, who acted as procurator in the Bach process, there were no theologians in Gregory's immediate circle who unconditionally supported his plans. In the end they had all thought of the sensation that the fulfilment of Gregory's wish must cause in the world. The world, after all, was no longer the Church's world it had been in the Middle Ages, when it really was easy to canonize people and it was possible to rely on the proposals of the devout and to put them into effect. Nowadays nothing but caution was called for. The Church had more enemies than friends. The tongues of the free-thinking and unbelieving élite of all peoples were adroit and ever ready to bear witness against Rome and its theologians. Voices had long since been raised dismissing Gregory's plan as nonsense; some had even said that the idea bordered on the cheap, as did so much about the Church. Now, while the process had become as good as dormant, this other movement had come into being, quite unexpected, surprising, a thing nobody had thought possible. And so Cardinal Hopkins regarded it as a miracle; the hearts of the free-thinking seemed more capable of enthusiasm than those of the faithful, especially of the theologians; and so far it was only the latter who had been consulted. Hopkins, overwhelmed by the prophetic powers of the Pope who had foreseen all this, told himself that the lovers of the world, whether Christian or not, would do just the same as those whom enthusiasm was now bringing to Rome to be near the dying Pope, were some future Pope to canonize a pair of great lovers on the grounds that their love had been a piece of sacred reality and thereby an ideal for all mankind. Those, however, who would emulate them—that was the point of canonization—must be agreeable to God. For God had created man after His own image and that meant that man should be creative. He had commanded men to love one another, and that meant that people should be fired with a pure love. That was in order. Those who were far off felt it, although they did not perhaps fully understand it. Who, however, did understand it, if not this sage whom the world possessed in Gregory?

Still Hopkins remained silent. He seemed ashamed to have such thoughts coming to him. Love and enthusiasm, hope and sadness, were hidden behind that sense of shame. And when Gregory asked him a second time why he thought these free-thinking people, musicians and intellectuals, men and women, students and art enthusiasts, wanted to come to Rome, he finally answered: "To pay homage to you, Holy Father."

Gregory smiled and gazed in front of him. Then he nodded and let his head with its brightness of silver hair incline to one side and shut his eyes beneath the magnifying lenses. Hopkins removed the glasses from that calm face, placed them on the little table, and walked away softly with bowed head.

CHAPTER 17

AMONG THOSE WHO CAME to Rome were Luise Hammerschmied and a number of her friends from the Hamburg
Cantata Society. The train rolled on toward its journey's end.
Luise was standing by the open window looking out at the
dusky countryside, where the lights of man were still wretchedly
ineffectual compared with the last great splendor of the evening
sky that was to be seen between the gray hills. The railway carriage had come from the shores of the North Sea, uncoupled
from various trains, coupled on to others, and so brought safely
to Rome. The travelers going to the Eternal City had been able
to entrust themselves to it without a care. The sound of the
wheels, of the axles, and of the wind, the gentle onward glide
down the incline between the hills, now announced the end of
the journey. Her luggage, her bag, and her violin in its case at her
feet, Luise leaned out of the window and looked across the fields
at the passing slopes, at the crests of the heights that were
crowned with the large dark shadowy buildings of the suburbs.
She heard her fellow passengers behind her naming the names
of the suburbs through which the train rolled, familiar names,
like musical themes often sought in memory. People began

making their final preparations for arrival, and meanwhile it grew darker and darker outside, and she had to put her head well through the window to avoid the coach's electric light and still be able to recognize things outside. Men and women, clergy and nuns, emerged into the corridor, brought their luggage to the doors, round each of which a little throng formed.

Excitement took hold of Luise, who was coming to Rome for the third time. She clasped the window frame to stop the trembling of her hands caused by the realization of entering the Eternal City. Her expectations were as great as ever. The circumstances of her first visit had been very similar. Then, too, it had been spring. She had come with many others in order, as now, to provide a feast of music. From the north, from the Hamburg to which Johann Sebastian Bach had made pilgrimage to the old master organist, Adam Reinken, the Cantata Society had set out on the trail of the music that the great masters had fetched from across the Alps several centuries before in order that it might be laid at the feet of Johann Sebastian. Rome has held the great treasure of Gregorian music; there Palestrina and Monteverdi had celebrated their solemn services. And Frescobaldi had crossed the country, going from city to city with ten thousand enthusiasts in his train. And now the enthusiasts were coming back to Rome, to pay homage to music, to pay homage to Bach, and—what was not put into words—to pay homage to the man who had pronounced both Bach and music saintly, music which, like love, contributed to God's law of creativeness; they were coming to pay homage to Pope Gregory who now lay dying.

The second time Luise had come to Rome had been two autumns before, when she was still under the influence of her first encounter with the city earlier that spring. She had come alone then; yet she had brought from the north those pictures that had adorned the walls of her Protestant theologian's home, among them one of the venerable Pope. She had remained in the city until, a year later, she had returned with her father to Germany to make propaganda for the Pope's great plan.

Many did the same. There were the monks who came to the places where Bach had worked in order to obtain material for the process in Rome; there were the lovers of music among the people who gave their support to Gregory's project. But, when the Pope fell ill, the men of Rome had gradually lost courage. Then new forces had arisen, prepared to help the Pope in his growing isolation. Yet it seemed already too late. The Pope would not rise from his bed again. So, in the end, came these free-thinking people, those who believed as well as those who did not, who had heard of each other and had long since founded an unofficial society for the furtherance of worthy causes. It was agreed that on Bach's birthday they would hold a festival in Rome, near Gregory, in order to show him and his theologians that the intentions of the invalid Pope were far from foreign to the music-loving section of mankind. It was difficult to say how it had all come about: it had begun here, found approbation and fulfilment there; now, as in the relay races of antiquity at Olympia, there was the goal, and thousands, tens of thousands indeed, were coming, pouring into Rome together.

The train came gently to a stop. Porters ran up, the motors of the little trolleys whirred; people surged and thronged. Luise Hammerschmied turned and nodded to her friends, still standing hesitant in the compartment, then looked out of the carriage door. People pressed past. Luise picked up her luggage and joined the stream. Then she was standing on Roman ground, and that urged her forward, as it were, ahead of the others, drove her along among noisy people and things, in a heavy expectant

seclusion of her own. In one hand she held her suitcase, in the
other her violin. This time she had not brought the pictures from
the walls, nor had she any music with her. After the festival it
was her intention to go back to Hamburg, where she ran the
Cantata Society. She had been able to persuade several of its
members to come with her to Rome and take part in the
concerts.

The little group entered the station hall. Huddled round their
baggage they stood and held counsel. They were kept busy
resisting the offers of the porters, hotel porters, and lodging touts
by whom they were continually being importuned. They nego-
tiated with one or two. Luise had neither eyes nor ears for what
was happening round her. She heard the newspaper men shouting, saw the agitated crowds of people at the kiosks. Slowly, like
a sleepwalker, she went across to one of the newspaper kiosks.
It was so closely besieged that she could not get through; she
was unable to see above the heads of the people, was thrust
back by those making their way through the dense throng with
their newspaper trophies in their hands, and suddenly she felt
a dark dread of further investigating the cause of the crowd's
agitation. When she got back to her companions they had come
to terms with one of the lodging touts, an old man: he was
going to take them to a *pension* on the far side of the Thermae.
Luise agreed, handed over her luggage to her friends, and
promised to join them there later, when she had roamed a bit
in the city.

Luise ran off alone into the city, whose walls she scanned with
eyes that were at one and the same time questioning and anxious. The lights burned as fixedly as ever; the gay neon lights
still snapped on and off, the tall spray of the murmuring fountains still glistened in the glare of the floodlights. Luise walked
across the square, again heard newspaper men shouting, saw

people gathered round the newspaper kiosks, saw various bright lights go out, saw shopkeepers putting up their shutters before the usual time. She saw copies of the special editions in every hand. When a string of buses that some traffic block had driven into a herd came to a halt by the curb, she got into one whose destination was given in red lettering—the cathedral of St. Peter's. She paid for her ticket, feeling ashamed at the readiness with which she had acted on this sudden impulse. She gazed avidly at the streets of the Eternal City which were even now changing over from commerce to the places of leisure that they became in the evening. Things had lost their definition in the faint light still coming from the few shops whose owners were closing them, one by one. Her hand hung loose in the leather strap above her; though it was meant to be grasped firmly, she could not hold it. The swaying of the bus made her feel giddy. The name BACH greeted her from some posters on walls, though the two Christian names, being in smaller type, were no longer distinguishable: but from the street corners the newspaper men were crying the name of the Pope. It was at that hour that the world heard of his death.

The bus stopped a few streets from St. Peter's. The passengers, most of them grasping black-edged evening papers across which was printed in large letters the name of the Holy Father and his bold Roman numeral, alighted in silence and were swallowed up in the dark space of the city on the far side of the Tiber.

A deep silence reigned over everything. The shops were shut. Hardly a car drove through the streets. On the far side of the colonnades it was almost dark. The great space in front of the cathedral of Christianity was empty, and in the pale light of the street lamps you could see groups waiting in silence, looking up at the black walls of the Vatican. No sound came from the fountains. People were going up the steps to the entrance of the church. The basilica had been opened and tiny lights were burning in praise of God who has the power to grant life after death. From beneath the dome of St. Peter's came the sound of singing:

Deus, qui potestatem habes
donare vitam post mortem.

ABOUT THE AUTHOR

JOHANNES RÜBER, born in 1928, has had three novels published in Germany; *Bach and the Heavenly Choir* is the first to appear in this country. He attended the University of Bonn, studied dramatic art at Düsseldorf, and has worked at various jobs—on a farm, in a newspaper office, for an insurance company, as secretary to a French author—to his present status as a writer. His greatest pleasure is traveling, and climbing mountains should he be near them. It was in Positano, in southern Italy, high on the cliffs overlooking the Mediterranean, where he found the idea for this book. In February of 1954 the present Pope was ill. The season was rainy, and a friend played Bach to pass away the hours. "All my thoughts about Bach united with the ill Pope," he writes. "At that time the Pope ordered all the works Bach had written for the organ to be played in the little church of St. Maria in Rome. So I gathered material for my novel." Johannes Rüber is married and lives in Munich, Germany.

THIS BOOK WAS SET IN

ELECTRA TYPE AND PRINTED AND BOUND BY

THE HADDON CRAFTSMEN.

THE PAPER IS PERKINS AND SQUIER COMPANY'S

RRR SMOOTH ANTIQUE

MADE BY THE P. H. GLATFELTER COMPANY.

TYPOGRAPHY AND DESIGN ARE BY

LAWRENCE S. KAMP